JUSTUS WALKEN

By L. Dean Lewis

INTRODUCTION

I hope you take something away from reading this book. While many of the things you read may seem like reality, this is a work of fiction. The sad truth for many is that parts of this book are not fiction, but their everyday lives. I sincerely hope one day that can change. This book is dedicated to everyone who has had to live with violence as a regular part of life.

Copyright 2007 L. Dean Lewis   ISBN 978-0-6152-0078-1

TABLE OF CONTENTS

"CAN'T YOU DO ANYTHING RIGHT?"

No! No! Please stop! I'm sorry; I didn't mean to upset you! The words echoed off the walls and up to my room where I huddled under the covers. This was definitely not the first night, and I knew it wouldn't be the last time that this nightmare would repeat itself. That was nearly 12 years ago and it is still vivid in my mind.

I suppose that night stands out in my mind since I decided at that point this had to stop. I had always hated what was happening and now that I was old enough I was finally going to do something about it.

Time passed very slowly back then to me, and at night, at least on the few quiet ones, I would lie in my silent room and imagine a way to make all of my nights peaceful like the one I was having. I really don't know when it all started; I guess there was always something wrong, at least in my dad's eyes. Mom would make the few dollars we had stretch and make creative yet inexpensive meals, but to my dad it was always "slop of the day". Even on the special occasions where we had some extra money and we could have a turkey at Thanksgiving, or a ham on Christmas, dad would find something wrong with the meal. Mom stayed at home and took care of the house and me, and I always thought everything was perfect, but not dad. He could find the smallest thing wrong and make a federal case out of it. "Goddammit woman, can't you even clean the TV screen? I can't even see the fucking game through all this dust!" I knew it was his chain smoking, not the dust, but this was typical, and eventually a cause for a slap or worse. Mom almost never went anywhere outside of the grocery store, or maybe the fabric shop, dad didn't want her to be seen if she was hurt, and if not, he didn't want her "whoring around flirting with every man out there". I never so much as saw mom talk to a man, let alone flirt.

So as the years passed the abuse got worse, until I was afraid for her life. Which takes me back to that night and the realization of what had to be done. The day before, some friends of mine and I had gone to see a movie called Death Wish, the man in the movie decided he needed to take the law into his own hands, and since it always seemed like the law wouldn't, or couldn't help my mom, I knew I would have to do it.

I think that movie, maybe more than any other thing in my life put me on the course that led me to where I am today. I don't regret anything, except perhaps that I couldn't be in more places at once.

From the moment I left the theater, I decided what had to be done; now I would just have to devise a plan.

"Hi mom."

"Where have you been?"

"Please don't tell dad, my friends and I went to the movie."

"Don't worry, I won't tell him." She gave me a little smile, enough that I saw it, but not enough to open the split on her lip.

"You look really nice today mom."

"Thank you James, I feel better too."

"When is dad coming home?"

"Probably after midnight as usual." She had a sad and yet fearful expression on her face and I knew that if he had a bad day at work, or a worse one at the bar shooting pool, she would be the one he took it out on. He had never really hit me much, I don't know why, maybe only because he didn't see me often enough. I of course got the same verbal abuse that my mom did and was continually told how I 'couldn't do anything right' or 'you are completely worthless' among a throng of other self esteem destroyers. I avoided being in the house when he was there and stayed at my friends' houses, the few that I had, or just outside as much as possible.

The start of deer season was only a couple days away and I had decided that I was going to go with him. It would be easy to get him to take me I thought, in his eyes all 'real men' hunted.

The next day I approached him cautiously and asked if I could go with him. He didn't smile or give any sign of approval; he just looked me in the eye and said,

"It's about time you learned how to do something a real man does." I turned and walked from the room and thought to myself "if you are what a 'real man' is, then I would rather be an animal."

Some say that is what I am now, but if so at least I am not my fathers kind of man.

The next morning I was woke up abruptly before the sun came up, "get up lazy, the deer don't keep bankers hours and if we want to kill one then we can't either." Yes I did want to kill something, and wondered why it didn't bother me more to think like that. I guess I had stopped thinking of him in any way other than he was a thing, a loud, drunk, violent thing that would kill the only person I loved if I let him. If he was in such a hurry I wouldn't disappoint him. I quickly pulled on my long johns and started to layer on the rest of my clothes as he was yelling at me to "get my lazy ass downstairs". I ran down and he met me at the bottom shoving a shotgun into my hands. "You took so damn long there is no time for you to eat breakfast" I didn't really care and was kinda sick to my stomach anyway. I walked out the back door behind him and felt the cold blast me in the face, I never knew a morning could be so cold, and I wondered if it was the cold outside, or the coldness I felt inside that made me shiver uncontrollably.

As we walked across the field I could hear him muttering to himself about what a waste of time it was taking me, and how he should have been out here hours ago. We finally reached the edge of the woods and he told me to stay put while he looked for some sign. I was glad he left and my shivering had finally stopped, as I sat there waiting I thought about what I was going to do. Suddenly he came up behind me.

 "What the hell are you doing?" I couldn't believe how I hadn't heard him coming and his words made me jump to my feet. "Sitting on your ass sure as hell won't get you a deer!"

"I'm sorry, I thought you wanted me to stay put."

"Yeah, but you could at least be standing up and looking for some game, I don't know how I got such a lazy son." With those words he turned and headed back to the woods. I stood there for a minute not sure if I should follow, but the mystery was soon solved "come on dammit, get your ass behind me and stay close. I haven't seen one goddamn track yet, where in the hell are all the deer?" After about a hundred yards he stopped and told me to stay put, he was going to walk up and around and try to flush something my way. I looked around and thought about where I would hide, seeing a large fallen tree I decided that was a good place to conceal myself. I crouched down and hid myself behind some branches and waited for what seemed like an eternity. I felt sick and my hands were starting to shake about the time I saw movement coming down the hill. He was very quiet and I wondered how he could be so stealthy, when most of the time he was loud and obnoxious. I couldn't stop my hands from shaking and for a minute I thought he would see the barrel of the gun as it protruded from the branches and shook with my hands. Suddenly the thought of him seeing me scared me to the point where I froze and the shaking abruptly stopped. It was starting to snow and for a moment he was obscured by the flakes, then as the shadowy figure came into focus I could see his face, the scraggly beard, clenched jaw, and eyes colder than the falling snow. I braced myself and thought of mom, how she needed me now and how if I didn't act it would be her funeral that I would be going to. I aimed the gun and held my breath, as I pulled the hammer back he suddenly turned and looked straight toward me! Had he heard it? Did he think I was game of some sort? A hundred things flashed in my mind as he looked straight in my direction, the next thing I knew there was an explosion and I fell backwards into the brush. Had I been shot? I couldn't move, I felt paralyzed and couldn't breathe. There was no pain and I didn't know what to do, but knew I had to try and get up to see what had happened. I slowly looked down to my feet, there was no blood on me and I was still breathing. Getting up I made my way to where I had been looking moments earlier. He was there, lying on his back with a splatter of crimson snow behind where he had been standing just minutes earlier. I felt like I would throw up, but since I hadn't eaten, all I did was dry heave until my throat hurt. I grabbed my gun and started running, I didn't know if he was alive or dead and just wanted to be as far from there as was possible.

CRASH! The glass shattered from the back door. "Oh My God!" My mom jumped up from the kitchen table as the glass sprayed across the floor, "what in god's name are you doing!? Your dad is going to kill you when he sees what you have done!"

At the moment all of this was taking place I didn't even think of the irony of her words, and since I wasn't even sure if he was dead all I could do was blurt out "dad has been shot!" She stared blankly at me for a moment, and then as if we were talking about the weather calmly replied, " Are you sure?" I was panting from running and still wanted to throw up, but kept on ranting.

"Yes mom, I saw him there on the ground."

"Ok, well I suppose I should call the sheriff." She calmly walked to the phone and began to dial, "hello, is this sheriff Clark? Hi, this is Betty Walken, James just came crashing through the back door shouting that his father has been shot." She continued to talk for a couple minutes, and then replaced the receiver and turned to me, "he said he would come over in a while and check it out. I had better get this mess cleaned up." I was somewhat surprised by the lack of urgency from the sheriff, and she seemed almost too calm considering the situation. I knew that my father was no pillar of the community, but you would think that a member of law enforcement would be a bit more professional.

I learned much later that my father had staged elaborate hoaxes in the past, to cover up things that he was doing behind my moms back, at least when he cared about what she thought. The last couple years he did whatever he wanted and didn't give a damn if she knew or not. As mom cleaned up the glass I noticed that I was soaked with sweat as a bead dripped off of my nose. "James, why don't you go change and I will make you something to eat, I am sure you are hungry by now." I should have been starving, I usually was, but right now all I could think of was the blood on the snow, him lying there, was he dead? Was he just wounded and would walk through the door at any moment? The thought of that made my heart race and I started to gasp for air.

"James, what is wrong with you? If you are worried about the door I will take the blame for it, it will be ok." She still didn't believe me, and now I was starting to wonder.

"Put the gun away and take off your wet clothes, I will make something to eat as soon as I am done here." I looked at the gun still in my hands and it suddenly occurred to me that there was a spent shell in it.

"Ok, mom I will." I walked to the basement door and down to where my father did his re-loading. Popping open the barrel of the single shot, I removed the shell and put it into the bucket with the rest, wiped the gun inside and out and took it back up to be locked in the gun cabinet. As I changed my wet clothes I looked out at the snow falling, it looked so pure and clean and I felt the desire to stand naked in it and wash myself back to the clean white that it was.

Just then the sheriffs car pulled into our driveway. I was now much calmer and would have to fake even caring now, I felt hollow inside as if all my emotions were suddenly dead. I pulled on my sweatshirt and ran down the stairs as I heard the knock on the door. Throwing open the door I yelled out, "my dad has been shot back in the woods!"

Sheriff Clark just looked at me, "ok son, let's get to the bottom of this. What happened?" I was nervous and started to shake, I wasn't prepared to answer questions right now; I thought he would just want to go back and see the body. "Uh... well... I was uh..."

"Calm down James" my mom said as she took my hand, "just tell the sheriff what happened."

"My dad told me to stay put and he would circle around to flush out some deer, I heard a shot and called to him to see if he got one, he didn't yell back so I started to walk toward where I heard the shot. I kept yelling so he would know it was me and not shoot me on accident."

" Well son, that's a good idea, then what happened?"

" I came upon a fallen tree and when I went around it he was laying in the snow and there was blood on the ground."

"Did you go over to him?"

"No, I was scared and didn't know what to do, so I ran home."

"Ok James, lets see if we can get back there and take a look around before this storm gets any worse."

"Bundle up James, I don't want you catching cold." Mom was always so worried about me, and it seemed odd to me that she would worry about me catching cold, when possibly her husband was cold and dead out in the woods.

The sheriff and I walked across the field as the wind whipped the snow around us; I couldn't even see the tracks from before and was disoriented by the snow blowing in my face. In the woods there was less wind and I thought I was heading in the right direction, but after what seemed like forever I still couldn't find the fallen tree.

"Sheriff, I know it's here somewhere, I just can't remember how to get there."

"Alright James, there is nothing more we can do at the moment, the storm is getting worse and the station is sure to be swamped with calls from stranded motorists and accidents. I need to get back." As we walked toward the house I kept having thoughts of him being there, standing in the kitchen with a bandage on his shoulder or arm with a gun in his hands.

"So James, you little bastard, trying to kill me huh?" He would say with an evil look in his eyes, "well too bad you were such a pussy and couldn't aim a gun! Now you are gonna pay like your mother already has!"

I could picture mom on the floor covered in blood just as the bullet from his gun went into my body. I let out an audible yell as the picture burned itself into my mind, and the sheriff turned to me and asked what was wrong.

"Sorry sheriff, I was just thinking about what happened today."

" It will be ok James, you'll see." He smiled at me and I knew that he was aware of the hell we had been through for so many years.

Finally arriving back at the house I could see my mom had taped some cardboard to the door to cover where I had broken the window in it. Sheriff Clark and I were covered in snow and tried to brush most of it off before we went in. Entering the kitchen my mom asked, "Did you guys find anything?"

"Sorry Mrs. Walken the snow is coming down too hard and James couldn't find where he thought your husband had been. When the storm passes I will bring a deputy and a dog and we will see what we can find then."

"Thank you sheriff, I appreciate you coming here and taking this time on such a miserable day." With that the sheriff left and mom closed the door.

"I made you some lunch, you have to be starving by now." I realized that I was very hungry and would be happy to have something warm to eat.

The hours passed and day turned to night, my mom sat in her chair and occupied herself with some sewing, but still she kept nervously looking up at the clock. I was enjoying the quiet and wanted to tell her it would be alright, that her peace would not be destroyed as it had been for so many years. Fatigue was slowly taking its toll on me and I found myself dozing off.

"James, go to bed you are exhausted." Her words startled me and I nodded to her as I got up and walked over to give her a hug.

"Mom, everything is going to be ok, I promise."

"I know James, you have always been the one to get me through the days, goodnight hun, I love you."

"Love you too mom, sleep well." with that I went upstairs and fell into my bed.

I wish I had been able to sleep well, but the night was full of demons that haunted my dreams. I saw over and over the red snow, the body lying there covered in blood, but in my dreams it would awake and chase me until I was caught and beaten into a shared grave. Finally morning came and I woke to the smell of food cooking and the sound of the wind still whipping the snow against my window. Walking down stairs the peacefulness of the house greeted me in a way that I hoped would last forever. I was sure by now that he would never come walking through that door and I would never have to hear my mom scream or cry again. I moved toward the kitchen and could hear my mom humming, it was the first time she had done that in years and I smiled as she turned to see me.

"Good morning sleepy head." She grinned at me and at that moment I knew I had done not only what I had to do, but that I had done the right thing.

I remember that day as being one of the best of my life up 'til then. We stayed in all day and watched the storm rage outside, she made hot cocoa and cookies, and even at seventeen I remember feeling like a little kid again.

The next day the storm passed and later in the afternoon the sheriff pulled into our driveway. Mom answered the door.

"Hello Betty, how are you doing today?" Sheriff Clark looked a bit worn out but smiled at my mom.

"I am doing well sheriff, James has been taking good care of me."

"That's good to hear, you know deputy Glass don't you?"

"Yes of course, how are you today Bill?"

"Doing fine ma'am, just gettin' the dog ready to do a bit of trackin'."

Bill had of course been to our house many times over the years, but I hadn't seen him lately since mom had given up and stopped calling the police when she realized that it just made things worse. At first dad would apologize, and beg for mom to forgive him promising that it would never happen again. He would cry and tell her he loved her and she wouldn't press charges, then after a while he would just threaten her, and tell her that if he went to jail that not only would she be sorry, but he would take it out on me. I felt guilty for years knowing that he was using me to manipulate her, but she loved me more than she loved herself and would do whatever it took to protect me. The sheriff broke into my thoughts just then.

"Alright, lets get going there are a million things I need to get done today."

"Ma'am?"

"Yes Bill,"

"Would you happen to have something Mr. Walken has worn recently?"

"Um, yeah, here take this old jacket, I don't think it has been washed in a while." She handed Bill the jacket and he let the dog smell it for a minute and then they were off across the field.

A couple hours later I heard a knock on the door.

"James, can you get that? I have my hands in the sink." I opened the door to see the sheriff standing there.

"Can you get your mom for me James?" Mom came up behind me before I could turn around and the sheriff asked her if they could speak alone for a moment. I went into the kitchen but listened by the door. He spoke softly but I could hear him saying that he radioed for the coroner and death was instant. I felt a wave of relief knowing he was really dead and then an evil thought that I wished he had suffered more, that he knew what it felt like to be in pain and to know he was going to die there alone in the snow. I heard the door close and mom came into the kitchen. "Son, you were right, your father is dead, he was shot through the heart and died instantly. The sheriff says they had a hard time finding the body and that finding out who did it will be nearly impossible. Things like this happen every hunting season he said and it will most likely just be written up as a hunting accident." I looked into her eyes as they started to fill with tears, as they ran down her cheeks I put my arms around her and she quietly cried. She pulled back after a minute and looked at me.

"James, you are going to think I am the most horrible person in the world for what I am going to tell you." I didn't know what she was going to say next, but I was thinking at that moment that I was the most horrible person in the world. "Son, I am not crying because I am sad, I am crying because I am relieved and because I am free." At that I started to cry, she just pulled me to her and we wept together. From that moment forward I knew I would never regret what I had done, I gave Mom her life back and she could once again be happy.

A REVELATION

I don't think I had ever seen my mom happy for so long, each day she would come out of her shell a little more, she would hum or sing to herself, have a friend over, even put on makeup. The best part was now she put it on because she wanted to, not to cover a bruise. She still only had a couple of friends, and my favorite was Janice. Janice worked at the fabric store and my mom had known her longest. For some reason they were really close and despite Janice being a number of years younger, it was like 2 schoolgirls when they were together. They would sit, talk and laugh for hours. Janice always seemed so sad to have to go home, and despite my mom urging her to stay for dinner she never did. I kind of developed a crush on her since she was so nice to me and I thought she was absolutely beautiful. She had short blonde hair and bright blue eyes that I would find myself staring at when I thought she wasn't paying attention to what I was doing. I felt awkward around her and if she caught me looking at her I would always say something dumb to cover up the fact that I was staring at her. I was happy that my mom had such a good friend and that she was able to do things and go places and not have to be alone.

The sperm donor that called himself my father had a good insurance policy at work that I didn't even know about, and this took care of the burial and gave mom enough money to be able to enjoy her life for a change. She wanted to get a job though and I thought it was great that she could go out and make money she could call her own. Janice got her a part time job at the fabric store and they became inseparable, which I really liked.

Time went on and I rarely thought of the killing and when I did I was glad I had done it.

I am sure that a person like you could never understand how it feels to kill, but I feel like I gave someone good a life and that is more important than anything.

I got part time work at one of the local farms, started saving money and one day I approached my mom and told her that I wanted to get my drivers license. Since the killing I had decided to quit school and be around home more to do the things that needed to be done, work, and just avoid people in general. I never really had any close friends since I wasn't allowed to have anyone over it was hard to get close to the other kids. I also found myself hating a lot of them for no reason except that I figured they had a normal life and I didn't. It is an irrational feeling I know, but when you become jealous of someone else's life, that is what can happen. So anyway, I missed the chance for drivers ed in school.

Mom was hesitant and told me that I didn't even have a car so what would be the point? I told her that I had saved quite a bit and could buy one if she wouldn't mind. She had the strangest look on her face and I didn't know what was wrong.

"Mom, are you ok?" she had that fearful look in her eyes that I hadn't seen for a while and I wondered what I had said to make that happen.

She took a deep breath and said "James there is something you don't know about yourself." What was she talking about? How could I not know something about me? Maybe I was adopted, that might explain why my "dad" never liked me I thought. As the thoughts raced through my mind she spoke.

"I have something to show you." Getting up she walked to her room and came back in a few moments with a locked box. "This has every important paper and a few keepsakes from my father and mother. You never knew them of course."

The only thing I knew about my grandparents on my moms side was that my dad hated them and they had been killed in a car accident while my parents were still dating. I never asked questions about them since it would just enrage my father.

She continued "You know I have told you some things about my parents, but not a lot I am sad to say. They were good people and never wanted me to marry your father, they hated him." I could guess why but my mom went on, "At first he wasn't the man that you knew, but he always drank a lot and they didn't like it, now for the things you don't know." She took a moment to collect her thoughts and I could see her eyes filling up with tears.

"James... I was pregnant before your father and I married, in fact I had you before we were." I just sat there and didn't know what to say, but it didn't matter to me really, I was still the same person.

"Mom, that's ok, I understand"

"I hope you do, but back then it was horrible for a woman to give birth out of wedlock, and then there was the accident and I was alone and scared. I wanted you to be the man your grandfather was, he was a kind, loving, decent man, and I named you after him." She handed me a piece of paper and said, "this is your birth certificate, you will need it to get your license."

I took it from her shaking hand and looked at it.... anytime my grandfather was mentioned he was "J. T." now as I looked at my birth certificate, I couldn't believe what I saw, "Justus Thomas" I was speechless and looked at my mom and the tears running down her face. "Son, I loved my dad and I love you. I hope you understand, your father hated the name and said all it did was remind him of cops, and he hated them. I was never allowed to call you Justus, and he forbid me to tell you."

"But he must have known that someday I would have to know."

"Yes but by then you would be an adult and he didn't care once you were out of the house."

"I understand, I just need some time to absorb all of this." She continued looking at me with sad eyes and I hated to see that.

"Mom, it's ok, it's not your fault and I am fine." I wasn't sure what to think actually as I walked upstairs looking at this piece of paper.

I guess no one can tell how they will react when they discover a truth that has been kept from them their whole life, I mean in a way it was no big deal, I could still be called James and I didn't have to tell anyone, but at the same time I was named after someone that was good and loved by my mom and the name obviously meant a lot to her. "Justus Walken" I said it out loud and thought about how it sounded, almost like a description of something more than a name. I pondered this and suddenly was aware of someone watching me

"Mom! Holy crap you scared me!"

"I am sorry son, I wanted to show you some pictures. This is your grandfather when he was your age." I looked at them and my jaw dropped, if she hadn't told me I would have thought they were of me. "You look a lot like him, don't you think?"

I continued to look at them and then finally nodded, "how come I never saw these before?"

"I had them hidden, I didn't want your father to see them and maybe destroy them. I have so little from my family and I couldn't take the chance." It was sad but true, I only had a couple relatives and they all lived quite a ways off.

"After the accident the family all kind of fell apart, your uncle and aunt blamed me I think since they were killed leaving my apartment and we had argued about me marrying your father. Son, I have always carried the guilt with me, and maybe it was my fault."

"No mom, it was not your fault, accidents just happen."

"I feel like their accident put me in prison, and your dad held the keys to it. Now I am out, if I was responsible in any way, I think I have paid the price."

She was right I thought to myself, she had been caged but it was never her fault. I took her hand in mine, "Mom, please call me Justus from now on."

JANICE

Time marches on inevitably and my 18th birthday was fast approaching. Mom had been working part time and I was now driving her back and forth to work. This was good for me, not only since I had a part time job at the store across the way, but I got to see Janice more also. Mom would always say that I didn't need to come into the store to let her know I was there, but I told her it was no big deal. Janice would always come over and talk to me while mom finished up and I wished time would stand still in those moments. We never really talked about anything, but nothing never seemed so important. I realized one day that I knew nothing about her and decided to casually see what I could find out from my mom.

"How was your job today?" Mom asked.

"Not bad, kinda boring I guess, I don't seem to have anything in common with the other kids that work there."

"You have always been mature for your age Justus, that might be it."

I still was getting used to being called Justus, but I felt more like a unique person and had never heard of anyone else with my name.

"I suppose so, they are always just talking about girls and cars, and I don't know much about either one!"

I laughed a little and mom did too.

"Girls just lead to trouble you know." She made a funny face at me and I had to laugh again.

"Some girls are nice, Janice is nice."

"Yes, but she is not a girl, she is a woman and there is a difference."

" Of course, but she is still a girl to me."

" Justus, there are some big differences, sometimes a woman has to do things she doesn't like, and has to put up with a lot of things that a girl would run away from."

"Like what?" I was not sure where this was going, but my mom took a serious tone of voice and I could tell something was bothering her. "Justus, life is not fair sometimes as you know, and I know you have a crush on her."

"What!? What do you mean? I do not!" Maybe I was a bit defensive, but I thought I was so clever and hid it so well.

"I am your mother, I know you better than anyone on earth, and I understand."

"Well she is really nice."

"Yes she is, but you don't know her like I do, and sometimes what you see isn't what is really there. Remember when you bought this car?"

"Of course I do."

"Think about how much you liked how shiny and good it looked? And it still does, doesn't it?"

"Of course it does." I rolled my eyes, since I knew what was coming next.

"Now how many times have you had it in the shop? 5, 6 times?"

"Yeah, I know, it needs some work, but it is a good car and like you said it looks good!" I put on my big fake smile and tried to figure out her point.

"People can be like cars Justus, they are all shiny on the outside, but there are problems you can't see."

"What do you mean mom?" I was getting annoyed and wanted her to tell me what she all of a sudden didn't like about Janice.

"Justus, don't get me wrong I love Janice she is a wonderful woman, but there are things you should know. For starters she is married." I almost swerved off the road when I heard this.

"WHAT! How can she be married?!! She comes over all the time, she doesn't wear a ring and she has never said a word about a husband!" I felt as if my world had just been deflated and I was sinking into a deep dark hole.

"She comes over all the time because he works a lot, he pawned her ring because money was tight, and she doesn't like to talk about him." Well that was to the point I thought, but I wasn't going to just let it go.

"But mom," she cut me off and said it was not something I needed to concern myself with.

This was the first time since the killing that Mom was so closed mouthed and we drove the rest of the way in silence. I felt so betrayed, how could Janice be so nice to me and seem like she liked me so much when she was married? I didn't even want to talk to her anymore I told myself, I wouldn't even go in the fabric store and wait for mom. I remember sitting out front and seeing her talk to customers smiling and being so friendly, I wondered if she even gave a damn that I didn't come in anymore.

I looked down at my music and put my new Boston tape in, then looked up and almost jumped, Janice was right at my window. "You startled me!" She laughed and joked about being scary without makeup.

"Why don't you ever come in to see me anymore?" she looked a bit sad, but I was still feeling hurt and wanted to be cold.

"Ask your husband" I sarcastically replied. She looked surprised at first then even sadder.

"I am sorry Justus, I didn't mean for you to think I was keeping a secret from you, but I never talk about him to anyone." At that she turned and walked back to the store. I immediately felt like a jerk and jumped from the car, or at least tried to, my seatbelt was still on and I must have looked foolish trying to get out while still buckled. By the time I got it off she was already in the store, I ran up and into the door, but she was not in sight.

"Justus, I am almost ready" Mom said as she caught sight of me.

"Mom, where did Janice go?"

"She just went in the back" I ran past my mom and she looked strangely at me as I hurried to the back of the store. The light was dim and I couldn't see anyone,.

"Janice? Are you back here?" I could hear something to my right and walked slowly as my eyes got accustomed to the light. "Janice is that you?"

"Justus, please go back out front" I could tell she was crying and I felt like a heel.

"I am really sorry, I didn't mean to make you upset." I walked closer to her, she had her back to me so I put my hand on her shoulder and apologized again. Abruptly she turned and put her arms around me, I didn't know what to do so I just stood quietly and held on to her. "James, sorry I mean Justus, I have never met any guy like you, you really care about peoples feelings and you aren't afraid to show yours."

"I guess, but sometimes when you have feelings they get hurt."

"I didn't mean to hurt your feelings, and I never lied to you, I just don't talk about some things."

"I didn't mean to upset you either, I hope you can forgive me."

At that she pulled back to look at me, wiped her tears off and smiled slightly,

"Of course, you are too special to me to let it affect us." I was glad and at that moment I heard my mom come in the back, "are you guys back here?"

"Sorry Betty, I didn't mean to leave you out front all by yourself." She said as she quickly pulled away.

"That's ok, I was just wondering if Justus was gonna take me home, or do an inventory back here!" She let out a little chuckle and it broke the tension.

On the way home it was unusually quiet. "Mom, why doesn't Janice talk about her husband?"

"Do you talk about how your car is a piece of junk? Of course not, you talk about the things that you like about it, that is the way life is sometimes. Do you think I ever talked about your father with anyone? No, but I always talked about you, I am proud of you, and Janice is proud of who she is, and no one wants to admit their mistakes."

"I understand, but if she knows it was a mistake why not get a divorce?"

"That son, is none of our business." She was unusually curt with me and I almost pushed the issue, but decided it was better to just drop it.

"Is she coming to my birthday party?"

"Of course, she is your friend isn't she? I also found out your aunt is coming into town, and she and her newest husband will be there as well." I loved the sarcastic way she said "newest husband" I think this was number 4 and I wondered why anyone got married.

"That will be nice, I like her. Not as if I have tons of friends or anything, so it is fine to just have a couple people there." I really only wanted Janice there now, but couldn't say that.

My birthday came quickly and I awoke to the smell of homemade cinnamon rolls. "Mmmm... Wow those smell wonderful" I said as I walked in the kitchen. "So how is the 'man' of the house today? Do you feel different?"

"Ha ha, sure mom I grew 4 inches last night and a beard, can't you tell?"

"Well you passed me up in the height department years ago, so I wouldn't have noticed, but please no beard!" She laughed and I assured her that would never happen! After breakfast I was helping her clean up when I heard a knock on the back door, mom went to it and I had to laugh when I saw Janice as she came in, she had a scarf and dark glasses and looked like Jackie O.

"Nice Janice, are you trying to be incognito?"

"No Justus, I just wanted a different look today, do you mind giving your mom and I some privacy?" Odd I thought, she never asked me to leave the room.

"Of course not" I walked upstairs making sure they could hear me and turned the radio on in my room. What was so secret I thought? Ok, I was still a kid in some ways and if they were talking about my present, I wanted to know what it was! I crept downstairs and peeked into the kitchen. I couldn't believe my eyes! Janice had the sunglasses off and she had a serious black eye. I listened as they talked.

"Betty, I know you are good with makeup and I don't want this to be so noticeable, I hope you can help me."

"Sure Janice, I can make it better, what did you do to deserve that?"

"I told him I was going to be home late because I wanted to come to Justus' birthday party."

"And he hit you for that?!! "

"Please don't say anything, if anyone asks I fell on my stairs, ok?"

"Of course Janice"

I was instantly enraged! I couldn't believe my ears or eyes, what the hell was going on here! Who hit her? I wanted to kill them right now. I stopped myself and went back upstairs. What had just happened? I really truly could have killed someone and I knew who it was without even knowing for sure. It was now painfully obvious, my mom and her had even more in common than I ever could have imagined. How could anyone be cruel to her? She was the most beautiful woman I had ever known and sweet and kind.. I could go on and on. But what scared me was that in an instant I could see myself again behind the barrel of a gun. There had to be something else I could do. I decided to go downstairs. "Mom, I hope you are done talking about my presents!"

I hollered as I walked to the kitchen. Walking in I looked toward where I knew Janice was sitting and saw her quickly put the sunglasses back on.

"Hey Jackie O, just love your new look!" I had to joke and smile so they didn't know that I knew what was going on.

"Ha ha Justus, who are you? Don Rickles?"

"No, I am much better looking!"

"Yes you are, and today you are a man, how do you feel?"

"Strangely I feel a bit older all of a sudden."

"Well you have been a man since I have known you, and have done a great job taking care of your mom, not that she needed it!" She winked at my mom and they both laughed for a second.

"Ok, I had better go and get ready for the party."

"See you in a bit" my mom and I both said in unison.

"I am going to make the cake now Justus, so make yourself scarce 'til the party."

"I am invisible!" and with that went outside to my car.

I loved to just sit inside of it and listen to music, I remember this day hearing a Steve Miller song, "Take the money and run" there was a lyric that said "he aint gonna let those two escape justice" and I had to think about this for a while. It seemed appropriate and I wasn't gonna let anyone escape Justus either.

Soon it was evening and my aunt and new uncle arrived, and shortly thereafter Janice. She came in and had put on some makeup but it was still obvious she had a shiner. My aunt, always a model of tact said, "what happened to your eye?"

Janice just smiled and told about how clumsy she was falling on the stairs and they both chuckled at this. I just smiled, but glared inside. The night progressed and I opened my presents and blew out the candles on the cake. My aunt brought out a bottle of wine and everyone had some, mom even let me have a glass.

"You know I don't encourage drinking, but you are a man today and this is a special occasion." I had drunk a few beers so I knew what a buzz was, but this wine was stronger and I was feeling it fast! Aunt Linda and her hubby left not much after that and it was just the three of us left.

"Betty, do you mind if I sleep on your couch? I have had a glass too many I am afraid."

"Of course not, will your husband be upset though?" This I didn't want to hear, "No he decided to go to Chicago tonight on 'business' "

"Oh yes of course, well it would be my pleasure to have you stay." The way she said 'yes of course' made me wonder what was up with that. My mom surprised me with what she next said.

"How about the 3 of us finish off this bottle of wine?" Mom almost never drank, and to offer me more was really a surprise. As she poured the last into my glass she said "A toast, to Justus and to freedom!"

"Hear, hear, to freedom" Janice raised her glass and clinked it to mine smiling and looking into my eyes. I felt a bit funny and wasn't sure if it was the wine, or something else. I was soon feeling somewhat dizzy and decided I should go to bed. "Mom, Janice, I think I need to go to bed, this has been a great day and night, thank you so much." As I got up mom gave me a hug and so did Janice.

"Good night Mr. Justus" and she winked at me.

I crawled into bed and wondered why it seemed to be moving, what an interesting sensation I thought as I lay there. All I could think about was how I felt, that I was melting into the bed, the light shining into the room from the full moon, the quiet, Janice standing there looking down at me.......what the hell?? "When did you come in?" She put her hand to my mouth.

"Shhhhh... You will wake your mom. I have something I want to give you on your birthday." I started to speak but she moved her hand and replaced it with her lips. I couldn't believe it, and put my arms around her neck. I was suddenly aware of my inexperience and turned my head.

"What's wrong Justus?"

"I haven't kissed a lot of girls, I am not good at it."

"Then think of it as part of your present, I will show you how to kiss."

"Ok, I...." my words were stopped by her mouth on mine.

She taught me more than how to kiss that night and I have never forgotten it, I guess it is just another reason I am here talking with you now, funny how life turns out.

CAN'T ESCAPE JUSTUS

It was just starting to get light and I felt Janice lying close to me. What had happened last night? I of course well knew but it all seemed like a wonderful dream and I was still afraid that I would wake up and that is all it would be. I moved slightly, Janice rolled over and put her arm around me, I could feel her breathing soft on my neck and didn't want to move again for fear this moment would end. My days this last week had been a roller coaster of emotions, finding out that she was married, and then that he mistreated her, were both depressing and infuriating. Then when I hurt her feelings I felt like the biggest loser in the world, but now, this was pure bliss for a change. As I was lying there thinking about how much had happened I heard a noise downstairs.

OH Crap! If my mom were up she would catch Janice up here with me, what would I say? What would happen then? I whispered to Janice to wake up, she softly mumbled something and continued to sleep. I whispered now,

"Janice, I think my mom is awake." At that she sat bolt upright and turned to look at me.

"Oh Justus, oh my god, I forgot I was even up here, I slept so soundly last night it was so wonderful. I have to get down to the couch somehow, or your mom will hate me."

"No I don't think she will hate you, but I am not sure how she would react to this, I doubt it would be with a smile and a cup of coffee!" I had to put a little joke and smile there for her so she wouldn't feel so bad, but as she got out of bed and began to dress I could see her back in the morning light. My mood went from light hearted to rage in an instant. Her back and the backs of her legs were nothing but bruises, I had never seen anything like it and I didn't know what to say or do. Should I ask her what had happened? I knew of course, any man that would blacken a woman's eye would have no problem hitting her where no one could see it. I decided to not say anything, but I knew exactly what I was going to do.

"Justus, do you think your mom is really awake?"

"I am not sure, I heard something downstairs, but just once."

She turned back to me now that she was dressed and I thought it was funny how she was now modest after what we had done last night.

"I am going to sneak downstairs, but I want to talk to you later when we have a minute alone."

She turned and crept out of my room and I wondered about the serious tone in her voice, was she sorry that she had come up to me last night? Maybe she was just drunk I thought, and it meant nothing to her. I know I was feeling the wine, but it didn't matter to me, I was elated that she had been with me and was glad that she had taken my virginity. I didn't hear anything from downstairs and assumed that my mom hadn't heard her come down, now I wanted to as well, and find out what was on Janice's mind, it was going to drive me crazy I was sure. After what seemed like forever I heard my mom.

"Janice, you are up early, did you sleep well on that old sofa?"

" I can't remember the last time I slept so soundly actually." I had to smile at this and got out of bed. Stumbling down the stairs I could see mom in the kitchen, and Janice still on the couch.

"Good morning son."

"Good morning Justus." Janice gave me a big smile and a wink as I looked toward her. I thought my face would crack at the big grin that was instantly upon it.

"Morning mom, morning Janice."

"Did you sleep well dear?"

"Wonderfully mom, I feel better than ever!"

"That's good, I imagine the wine had something to do with that!" she chuckled a bit and added how since now I was a man it was ok this time.

"Betty, I am going to have to get back to the house, I am not sure what time Bob will be home, and I don't want him to think I didn't sleep there last night."

"Oh Janice, I am sorry to hear that, but I understand."

"Justus, I hope you had a happy birthday, and have a great day today." She smiled broadly at me and went out the door.

"I sure do like Janice, she is always so nice to you."

"She sure is mom, I am glad she is your friend."

If she only knew...A few minutes later there was a knock on the door, and before I could get it Janice peeked her head inside,

" Betty, my car won't start, do you think Justus could give me a ride back to the house?"

"Janice, that old car of yours, I think it is worse than the one Justus is driving!" They both looked at me and laughed, and all I could do was shrug my shoulders and agree.

"I don't mind mom, I will eat when I get back, it is only a couple of miles."

"Ok, just hurry up, I made some biscuits, and they will get cold." I turned and followed Janice out, I was looking at her from behind thinking about the bruises on her, but then couldn't help think about how cute her body was, she was so petite, and I thought of how I held her close to me just hours before.

"Justus, I hope you don't mind driving me back to the house."

"Of course not, I was hoping to get to talk with you alone anyway." She turned and smiled at me and then we were off.

I had been past her house a number of times, I knew how neat and tidy she was, and yet the outside of it was a mess. There were a couple of cars that looked like they hadn't been moved in years, the paint was all peeling off and the yard looked like it was mostly just weeds and beer cans. We pulled in the driveway and she started to apologize for the way the place looked, explaining that Bob had told her the outside of the house was his job and he didn't give a damn if the neighbors liked it or not.

"It's ok Janice, it doesn't matter to me, I still like you."

"Ha ha Mr. sarcasm... well you can come in for a minute if you like." We walked up the porch steps and she told me that Bob probably wouldn't be home for hours, when he went to Chicago he was always slow in coming back.

"To tell you the truth Justus, I am pretty sure he has a girlfriend there." I was not surprised to hear this; men like him usually cheat on their wives. It occurred to me that she had cheated on him with me, I didn't care and wished I could rub it in his face, but I had other plans for him. As my eyes got accustomed to the dim light in the house I could see how much better it was inside than outside. The furniture was somewhat old and a bit worn, but it was all clean, except for one chair in front of the TV that had a ashtray full of cigarette butts, a bottle of whiskey and a pile of newspapers on the side of it. She saw me looking at it and told me that was "his chair" and she didn't touch anything around it. Then she walked up to me, leaned in and kissed me.

"Justus, I know you are not stupid, a bit naive, but not a fool. Bob is a mean and violent man; if he found out about us you would be in danger. The problem is, I have enjoyed my time with you so much, you are the exact opposite of Bob in every way, tender, compassionate, kind, and now after last night....I think I am in love with you." I was stunned, I stood there like a fool and didn't know what to say or do. She started to turn away.

"I shouldn't have..." I cut her off, turned her back to me and kissed her. She wrapped her arms around me and I have never felt so good.

"Janice, I have never had a girlfriend, my life has been kind of a mess and I just didn't want to start caring about someone, but getting to know you and spending time with you has been the best in my life, I find myself waiting for the time when I will get to see you, and then when you have to leave I miss you. The only person I have ever loved is my mom, until now. I hate that you have to be here, I love you too and I want you with me all the time." She began to cry, I pulled her against my chest and we stood there together.

"Justus, you know that can't happen, I am married and afraid of what would happen if I were to leave him. You know what he is capable of." She looked up at me and her eyes were filled with shame and sorrow.

"It's ok, I understand, everything will be alright, I promise."

"I wish they would, but reality is that I am trapped here when he is around. He will be home later, and is going to be pissed that my car is dead at your house. You had better get back home, your mom is going to wonder where you have been for so long." She was right; it had already been more than half an hour.

"Janice, it will be ok, you will see."

Kissing me one more time then turning me to the door "get outta here you dreamer, but your positive attitude is just one more thing I love about you!"

Smiling, she closed the door behind me. We would be free, both of us to be together, and she would never have to be hurt again, I would see to it, or die trying.

"Well Justus, that took long enough!"

"Sorry mom, but you know my car, it got hot and I had to pull over for a minute and let it cool down." I hated lying to my mom but didn't want to arouse her suspicions.

"So, what are your plans today son?"

"I was thinking of just hanging around here maybe working on my car a little."

"Alright, I have to go to town for a while, do you need anything?"

"Not that I can think of, thanks though" I really liked that she could go where she wanted and do things she enjoyed, now it was time to give Janice the same freedom.

Under the sink I knew there was rat poison, hmm... strychnine, I remembered in school how they said this was a powerful poison and would cause severe pain in the muscles and eventually death. I liked the idea of causing Bob severe pain. Mom had left and I had to figure out how to get the poison in the whiskey bottle by Bobs chair. I decided to call Janice.

"Hi Janice, can I come back over for a minute? I think I lost five dollars in your yard when I took my keys out." She said yes of course, but to hurry up in case Bob came home. Pulling into her driveway I was glad the yard was so overgrown, it would be hard to find anything in that mess.

"Justus you silly guy, how could you lose money in this neatly trimmed yard?" We grinned at each other and she came over and put her hand in mine for a second, then instinctively pulled back and looked around.

"Sorry Justus, I am never sure if Bob is around it is hard to not be afraid."

"Its ok, I understand. Help me look, do you mind?"

"Of course not it's nothing, and I would do almost anything for you." I just loved to hear her words and the sound of her voice was like music to me.

"Ok, then how about letting me use your bathroom." I said with a grin.

"It's the door on the right as you walk in, just hurry." I ran up the steps and into the house, going straight to the whiskey bottle I dumped the ground up pellets into it and shook it up. I hoped they would dissolve or I was screwed. Fortunately the bottle was a dark brown and it was hard to see if there was any discoloration. I held it up to the light and looked out the front, Janice was still looking around and I could see that the bottle seemed to not have any bits floating in it. Recapping it and putting it down I ran back out the front door.

"Was your mission a success?" she goaded me.

"A total success!" she laughed at me and I thought how I sure hoped it would be.

"I can't find anything in these weeds Justus, I am so sorry."

"Geez, don't worry it is only five bucks! I think I will live."

"You had better run, Bob could be home anytime. I imagine that we will be over later to try to get the car running."

"I will look forward to seeing you, but not Bob!" Glancing down the road she gave me a quick kiss, and ran back to the house.

"Goodbye for now baby!" and with that shut the door behind her.

I drove home in silence thinking about what I had done, would she find him and call an ambulance before he died? If he went to the hospital, he would know someone tried to poison him, then would think it was her! I would have to make sure that didn't happen. I walked into the house and to the gun cabinet, the box in the bottom had a revolver in it, and I would somehow make sure he never laid a hand on her again. I hid the gun under the drivers seat and went back inside.

Mom came home a while later, then shortly after dinner another car pulled in. I looked out and saw Janice getting out of the passenger door, then a big man got out of the driver's side. He was easily a foot taller than her and much bigger than me. I could see how she would be intimidated by him. He walked straight over to her car and opened the hood as she walked up to the house. My mom met her at the door and invited her in, she said no that he might want her help but she wanted to say hi quickly. I walked up behind my mom.

"Hi Janice, are you guys gonna fix the car?"

" I sure hope so, he is mad at me and says it is not running because I don't take care of it. "Turning back toward the driveway, I followed her.

"Maybe I can help." She didn't answer but as we approached the car just said, "Bob, this is Justus, maybe he can help." He looked up at me from under the hood, then looking back at her just said "if he knew anything about cars he should have fixed it already, give me another beer, I can do it myself." I wasn't sure what to say.

"Uh, ok, well if you want anything I will be in the garage. I wanted to be close enough to hear, but not let them know I was listening.

"This is not an engine, it is a grease pit! This car is a piece of shit, I should push it off a cliff. Did you get the oil changed?"

"No dear, I didn't have the money for that."

"You had better hope the motor is not seized, get in and try to start it." The car just kept cranking and wouldn't start.

"Goddamn piece of worthless shit! What the fuck did you do to this thing?"

"Nothing dear, I just came over this morning to give Betty some patterns and then it wouldn't start."

He worked on it for a while spending more time drinking beer than actually doing anything productive.

"I am sick of working on this pile of shit, I am going home, you had better figure out a way to get it going and be home before I go to bed, or you will be sorry."

At this I walked out, "any luck?" and before they could answer I volunteered "I have a friend that is a whiz at working on cars." It was a lie of course; I just wanted him out of there.

"I hope he is worth a shit" he bellowed as he got back in his car and drove out of the driveway.

"Oh Justus, I hope so, if I don't get this running and home..." her words trailed off and she looked at me as if someone had just sentenced her to death.

"Don't worry darling, I will take care of it." A half smile came to her lips, and she said how nice it was to be called 'darling'.

"I will call a friend, lets go in."

She quietly took my hand for a moment and we walked to the house. I dialed a random number and got a busy signal.

"Hey Curt, a friend of my moms car is dead in the driveway, do you think you can come over and look at it?... sure, in an hour? Ok, I will come pick you up then." Turning back to Janice and my mom I told them he could come over in an hour but he needed a ride.

"Who is Curt?" mom asked.

"Just a guy from the store, he wants to be a mechanic and is pretty good." Man I was such a huge liar, but I would do whatever it took to be able to be with Janice. I wanted to make sure I gave Bob enough time to get drunk and hopefully poisoned before I went over there.

After about an hour had passed I told them I was going to pick up Curt and took off. Driving toward Janice's house I reached under the seat and put the gun on my lap, if I had to, I would shoot him too.

I never had a regret about killing my 'father' but never thought I would consider doing it again. Now here I was, ready to take another life, funny how this time I was not shaking, in fact I was very calm. I parked down the road a few hundred yards and ran in the darkness toward the house. It was pretty dark and for a minute I wasn't even sure if he was there, but then a dim light shone through the front window. Quietly I snuck up the steps and peered through the corner of the window I had looked out of earlier today. I could see him from the side watching TV the bottle was on the floor and he appeared to be twitching. I put the gun in the belt line behind my back and slowly walked to the door. It was unlocked and I silently walked in, now I was nervous, he was so much bigger than me if he came at me I would have to be quick, I decided to just hold the gun behind me. I walked closer and could hear his labored breathing, there was a odd guttural sound to it and he seemed to be having muscle spasms. I decided to quickly move to where he could see me and kept the gun behind me. I could tell he was startled, but just barely moved his head to look at me. His mouth opened but his words were slurred and incomprehensible.

"What's wrong?" I said with thick sarcasm "are you in pain?" He just slowly blinked and I could tell he wanted to get up. "I know what you are, you are a piece of shit," with this I pulled the gun out, his fists tried to clench and his eyes became full of hate, anger, and then just pain." You will never hurt Janice again; you will never hurt anyone again. I hope you are in a great deal of pain, I hope you now know what it is to hurt. Your wife is in love with me, I made love to her last night, and am going to have her with me forever."

All of his muscles seemed to tighten up at this and I thought for a minute he was going to get up, instead he just stopped moving and I couldn't tell if he was breathing anymore. "Good riddance asshole" I lit one of his cigarettes, dropped it down on the stack of newspapers then lit them with the match and put it in the overflowing ashtray. The flames started to burn across the paper and toward the chair. I looked around for a minute and wondered if there was anything that Janice would have wanted not destroyed, but it was too late to think about that. Charging out the door I ran as fast as I could back to my car, I was glad there was no moon and this road was off the beaten path. It occurred to me that is probably how he was able to abuse her for so long and no one ever knew it. I drove slowly past the house and could see flames through the front window. "I hope you burn in Hell too!" I accelerated and drove quickly back home.

AN END AND A BEGINNING

"Where is Curt?" Mom asked as I came in the door, 'Oh crap' I thought, I completely forgot about fixing the car!

"Uh, he said that he wouldn't be able to come over until later, but he would take care of it."

"Justus, if I am not back home pretty soon Bob is gonna be mad at me."

"Don't worry dar…Janice, I will take the blame for you." I had to catch myself as I almost called her darling in front of my mom.

"I am sure you would, but you saw how he was tonight, he already had at least a 6 pack before he went home, and with a game on tonight he will probably drink more. He won't listen to anybody at that point."

"Janice honey, don't worry, Justus and I will go with you if you want maybe that will help." I think mom knew deep inside that there was no reasoning with a drunk abusive man, but she had to say something. I wanted to tell her it was going to be alright, that no one would ever harm her again, but all I could do was stand there and wait to see what would happen next. I tried to just seem normal, pretending to wait for a friend that didn't exist, to act like I had no feelings for Janice and to put it out of my mind that her house was probably burning down as I sat there. Mom made something for us to eat and I attempted to make small talk with Janice. I could tell she was upset and I was still a bit flustered, wondering how long it would be until someone saw the flames, just then my question was answered.

"Son, do you hear sirens?" The sound was growing louder and as I walked to the front of the house a police car sped by, a minute later a fire truck in hot pursuit.

"My goodness, what do you think is going on?" Before I could answer, another siren could be heard and soon blasted past the house.

"Let's see if we can find out where they are going!"

I was surprised my mom wanted to find this out, but she had lately seemed to enjoy anything exciting. I wasn't sure it was a good idea since I knew, but sooner or later Janice would find out.

"Yeah Betty, lets go see, I can't stand just sitting here anymore

"Justus, maybe you should wait here for your friend."

Crap, I couldn't do that..."Oh, it's ok I can take a quick ride and see what is going on with you, are you gonna drive mom?"

"Sure, my car is big enough that we can all sit in the front." And with that we were out the door. Janice was so cute, she took any opportunity to touch me, or just look at me and give me a knowing glance, and as we walked out she put her hand in mine. In that darkness I felt like we were the only two people on earth for a second. She climbed in and sat between mom and I, as we started down the road I felt her hand on my thigh.

"Look at that! You can see the light from a fire from here, that is toward your house Janice what else is over there?"

"Mostly just woods, someone must have started a brush fire."

We continued toward the light and as we drew closer I could feel her hand tighten on my leg.

"Oh my god......"

"Janice that's a house, is it yours?" Mom cut her off before she could finish.

"Oh my god," she repeated herself "it's my house!"

Mom slammed down the accelerator and in a moment we skidded up behind the fire truck. Running toward the fire we were stopped by a fireman.

"You can't get any closer"

"That's my house!, let me go!"

"Ma'am there is nothing you can do right now, just let my men do their jobs." I could see that the entire front part was destroyed and the fire was working its way toward the back rapidly.

"These older houses are hard to get under control" he continued "and they burn very hot, but we are going to do our best to save what we can."

"Janice, it will be ok, you and Bob can stay with us as long as you need." My mom put her arm around Janice and at that moment realized she hadn't seen him.

"Fireman, where is Bob? He lives here too." Mom had to repeat herself before the fireman heard her.

"Ma'am, there is no one here but us and the sheriff, who is Bob?"

"He lives here, his car is in the driveway, I'm sure he must be here!" At this the fireman ran toward the men fighting the blaze.

"Men!, there might be someone still inside! Has anyone been able to go in?"

"No sir," one of the men yelled back over the sirens still blaring, "the fire is too hot, some men tried to get in the back, but the smoke was too thick." Just then there was a loud explosion.

"Back up men, there could be more!" He came running back to Janice, "is there anything in there that could continue to be explosive?" Janice just stood staring at the fire.

"Janice" I patted her cheek, "Janice, did you hear him?"

"Oh god, I am sorry... yes he reloaded ammo, there are a couple large cans of powder in the back of the house."

"Men! Get back away, there is gunpowder and ammo in the back rooms!!" They were aiming the hoses toward the back just as another explosion tore through the wall, but this time there were the pops of ammunition going off as well. "GET DOWN!"

The firemen dropped the hoses and dove for cover as the shells exploded in an eruption of deadly projectiles. We all were on the ground as the top floor fell into the first one.

"I am sorry ma'am, I can't risk the lives of my men to save this house, I hope you understand." She just nodded and I could see her cry as the light of the fire blazed on.

"It's not as if I had a lot anyway, but now I have nothing"

"You have us, Justus and I will do anything we can for you, you can stay as long as you need to." I put my hand on hers and said it would be ok, and I would do whatever she needed. Looking up at me she had half a smile and thanked me as she took hold of my hand. We laid on the ground as the fire raged, the explosions finally stopped and the firemen once again trained their hoses on what was left of the house.

"Betty, I didn't expect to see you over here." Sheriff Clark then turned to Janice, "this will take a while to sort out, do you have somewhere to go tonight?"

"Yes sheriff, I am going to stay at the Walken's house."

"That's good, we will be in touch as we determine what happened here tonight. You might as well go now."

She nodded feebly and we all walked back to the car.

"Mom, Janice can sleep in my room, I will sleep on the couch."

"Justus, that is sweet, but I don't want you to give up your room for me."

"Janice he is right, you have no privacy in the living room, and tomorrow we can clean up the sewing room and find a bed somewhere for you to sleep on in there."

"You are both too kind, I don't want to be a burden though"

"Janice, mom and I don't consider you a burden in any way, you should know that!" I squeezed her hand as I said this and she put her head on my shoulder. I wasn't really too concerned that mom would think anything about this considering the circumstances.

"Janice, do you think Bob was home?" She had a bit of trepidation in her voice and I was curious as to how Janice would respond.

"Betty, I know you understand how I feel, maybe more than anyone and I hope you don't think me heartless, but... I could care less."

"Unfortunately, I completely understand." And with that we drove the rest of the way in silence.

Going into the house my mom broke the silence.

"Whatever happened to your friend Justus?"

"I guess he didn't show up"

"Well at least I don't have to worry about getting the car home!" Janice made a little laugh and we both did as well.

"I can make some dinner and we can all clean up. Justus, maybe you can get your room set for her while I get started cooking some dinner."

"It's ok Betty, he doesn't have to do anything special for me I am sure his bed is fine just the way it is." She looked at me and we shared a knowing smile.

"You know there is a place in town that will probably have some clothes for you, they have helped other people I know in time of need. I can take you there tomorrow if you like."

"Thank you Betty, I would appreciate it. I would like to take a shower though if you don't mind."

"Of course not, I don't have much, but I can get you some nightclothes and a robe if you like." With that they walked out of the room.

Later, after dinner we all sat around discussing the events of that night, it all seemed surreal, here I was with the woman I loved and she didn't have to leave. I sat and thought about this and saw Janice steal a glance or two in my direction.

"Betty, Justus, I am really beat, I think I am going to go upstairs now."

"Yes I am too Justus, it has been a long day."

"Goodnight Janice, goodnight mom." And I was alone.

I lay there on the couch for a while, thinking about everything that had happened. I felt no remorse for what I had done, and all I wanted was to go up to Janice. After about half an hour I decided to sneak up there.

"Janice, are you awake" I spoke in a barely audible whisper and doubted she would even hear me.

"Yes of course I am, come here. I couldn't go to sleep tonight alone." She pulled me to her and held me tight. "Justus, I am so mixed up and my emotions are a jumble.

I'm free if he is gone, and I can be with you, but at the same time I can't. If your mom knows about us it will probably destroy our friendship and I might lose you too."

"Janice I will do anything for you, you know that, and my mom isn't going to find anything out."

"Come, get in bed, I want you close to me." I took off my clothes and got in with her.

"I just want to hold you Justus, I hope that is ok with you." I pulled her close and didn't say a word as she slowly drifted off to sleep.

TRANSITION

I woke before dawn and slipped out without waking her, lying on the couch I wondered what was next. Suddenly I could see someone standing at the door, before I could move they came in, in the dark I couldn't see anything clearly but knew they were walking toward me. Whoever this was frightened me, I felt like the boy I once was hiding as my father came toward me. I was paralyzed with fear and wanted to yell but I couldn't. I smelled a sickening burning odor, and then heard a voice.

"Did you really think you could kill me so easily? Now you are going to suffer!"

OH My God, how could it be? How could he still be alive? My fear now made me move and I hit the light switch above my head. The sight in front of me was horrible, his clothes were badly burned and in some places you could see the burnt flesh hanging from his body, his hair was gone and his face black and bloody in a grotesque fusion. I finally found my voice and screamed at the top of my lungs.

"Justus, are you ok?" I turned to see my mom sitting in her chair with a cup of coffee. "You must have been having a nightmare, your scream almost made me drop my coffee into my lap!" I was soaked with sweat and my hands were still shaking, as I feebly replied that I was ok.

"Well, we will just have to get that spare room done today so you can be back up in your own bed, we don't want anymore nightmares!" That was the understatement of the year, I swear I could still smell the smoke as I struggled to regain my composure. Janice appeared at the bottom of the stairs and asked if everything was alright.

"I thought I heard someone scream."

"Justus was having a bad dream."

"Are you ok?" I looked at her thinking I must seem foolish to be so disheveled from a dream and told her of course I was, it was just a stupid dream. But in my mind I wondered, was it possible that he could have gotten out? Maybe when the fire got to him he woke up and got out the back. I started to feel like I should have just shot him, to make sure, but that would have been obvious even after a fire. It was ok, I was sure he was dead....at least I hoped so.

The day went by uneventfully as we worked trying to get the room ready for Janice. I heard a knock on the door and went to it.

"How are you today Justus?"

"Fine sheriff, do want to talk to my mom?"

"Actually I was hoping Janice Ryan was here."

"Um ya, just a minute." I called for her and the sheriff walked outside with her. A short while later she came back in, mom and I looked at her as she told us they had found the body in his chair. They were going to investigate further, but it looked as if he had fallen asleep with a lit cigarette and started the fire himself. My mom got up and hugged her, then I did as well.

"Janice are you ok?"

"Of course Betty, I just have to try to figure out what I am going to do next, my life has taken a one hundred and eighty degree turn and it is a bit overwhelming."

"I completely understand, just remember we are here for you."

I wanted to always be there for her, but at the moment I only agreed with mom and let it go.

I think back now how the time went so fast after that, they confirmed he had died in an accident, she got her homeowners insurance and another policy he had from his work. She sold the property with the burned out house on it, which was bulldozed under by the new owners. I remember one night how she said she was glad it was completely gone, and how knowing the place didn't exist anymore made her feel better. There was nothing that she cared to look for in the rubble, and never even went down that road again.

We would spend our days working, and many nights make love until we would fall asleep in each other's arms. I never felt so complete and the evils of my past disappeared.

About 6 months later everything changed.

"Justus, I need to talk to you." She had a serious look on her face and I thought she might start crying.

"What's the matter? Are you ok?" Putting her arms around me she started to sob.

"Justus....I have to leave here."

"That's ok, I knew you would get a place of your own soon, it will give us more time to be alone together." It was quiet for a long time as she continued to weep on my shoulder.

"No Justus, I mean I have to move away from here." I pulled back and looked at her face.

"What?! Why would you have to do that???" I felt a lump in my throat and suddenly felt ill.

"I can't stay here, we can't continue like this. You still have so much to do, to learn, so many life experiences still await you. I can't have you do what I did and get married so young, to never live your life while you have freedom."

Even though we had never said anything about marriage I had always imagined it would happen some day.

"I don't need to do anything or go anywhere, I am happy with you, I love you and don't want anything else." I could feel the tears rolling down my cheeks and wanted to turn away.

"Justus, look at me, you know I love you too, and that is why I have to do this for you."

"What, break my heart? Make me miserable and alone again?"

"No, give you the freedom to enjoy your youth, I feel that my youth, and my innocence is long gone, you still have yours."

"I am not so innocent" All the things I had done came to me in a flash and I wanted to say something, but just kept crying.

"Compared to me you are, you really don't know a lot about me, my past is not so great."

"I don't know what you are talking about, I DO know you and no matter what you have done I don't care!"

She proceeded to tell me, how she had been with a lot of guys, had an abortion, was arrested for stealing a car, and how Bob had gotten her pregnant and pretended that he wanted children so she would marry him. Finally how she lost the baby because of the beating he gave her so that she would miscarry. "The doctors told me I could never have children after that. Someday Justus you will meet a woman that is not damaged, you are a wonderful man, and you deserve a wonderful woman." She began to cry harder at this point and got up and ran to her room. I was stunned and sat there weeping like a baby as everything in my world fell apart. Mom drove up as I sat there, I got up quickly and turned toward the bathroom as she came in.

"Justus, can you help me bring the groceries inside?" I choked out I would in a minute as I walked into the bathroom. Trying to regain my composure I wiped the tears from my face, I knew mom would ask why both of us were so upset and I couldn't let that happen. I almost wanted to tell her though, to let it out in the open and maybe Janice would change her mind, but if not then I would have only made things worse. Why did this have to happen? Why couldn't our love be enough.

Now as I sit here I have thought a lot about love, I don't think it exists for many, but if so, it eventually is broken at the end of some ones life. I suppose that is an eventuality for us all, and I am glad I have had the privilege of knowing true love.

Janice told my mom that she was leaving that night, that she was moving a couple hundred miles away but that she would call and visit when she had the chance. Mom cried at losing her friend, and I just cried on my bed and wished I was dead as I listened.

The next morning I listened as Janice walked in and out of the house, she still had very little and it easily fit in the car she had purchased a few months back. Mom had gone to work early since they had given her more hours to cover the ones Janice gave up. I was alone upstairs when she walked in. "Justus, do you hate me now?" I turned away and felt my face get warm and my eyes tear up.

"No, I love you" I choked out.

She came up behind me and put her arms around my neck, I felt her warm tears drip on my hair, "I love you too, and I always will. I hope you never forget me."

"How could I ever forget you? You made my life feel as if it were worth living, I didn't know what joy was until you, how can you go?"

"Someday you will understand how much I love you Justus, please believe me." I turned around and held her to me as I had so many times, only this time my heart was breaking and I couldn't stop crying. After a while she kissed me, pulled away, and said goodbye.

A NEW ROAD

I threw myself on the bed and sobbed. How could she leave, what had I done? I didn't want to believe this was happening, only that things could go on the way they had been, and I could be happy for once in my life. I heard mom come in a while later but didn't want her to see me. So stayed upstairs, after a bit of time had passed she called up to me.

"Justus, are you up there?" I weakly answered that I was, but was feeling sick and wasn't going to be down for dinner. She asked if she could bring something up, and after trying to persuade me for a few minutes told me that she hoped I felt better soon. I drifted in and out of sleep all night and my dreams tortured me again as they hadn't for months.

I plodded through my life the next couple of weeks not really caring if I ate, worked, or anything else. Mom started to worry about me and told me I should go to the doctor, but I refused and said I would be fine. One morning I woke up and decided I needed to do what Janice said. I had to go somewhere else, someplace that I wouldn't have to see things everyday that reminded me of her.

That night I told my mom I needed to get out in the world and see some new places, and meet some new people. I expected her to argue with me, but surprisingly she told me how that might be a wonderful experience for me, and that she had always wanted to travel. I knew she had never even left the state, and now she told me how it might be fun to live vicariously through me.

"Justus, I don't want you to worry about me, with Janice gone I have lots of hours at the store and have made some good friends. I can actually have people over and do things that normal women get to do!" She smiled broadly at me and I was happy at that moment, reminded how I had given her the chance for a normal life.

"Mom, I am glad that you are ok with this and you won't just be sitting around alone all the time. I will write you all the time and call when I am able to."

The next morning I put what few clothes and things I needed in the trunk of my car, kissed my mom goodbye and took off. It felt strangely good to be out on the road, to start seeing new sights, I focused on looking ahead and trying to put behind me all of the drama and sadness I was used to. Sometime after noon I drove through a small town a couple hundred miles south of home.

There was a little diner on the main street and I was hungry. Walking in I noticed the place was empty and wondered if they were even open.

"OH, you startled me, I didn't hear you come in!" The waitress said as she came out from the kitchen. "The lunch rush is over and it is usually dead in here until dinner time."

"Sorry about that, can I get something anyway?"

"Of course, what would you like?" I sat and chatted with her for a while and enjoyed the food and the freedom I was experiencing. I told her about the journey I had just started and as I left she told me to drive carefully and enjoy myself.

I spent the next month or so going from place to place seeing things and meeting people. I stopped in and visited the few relatives I had and then kept on going. Janice was still on my mind a lot of the time, but I was beginning to see that she was right and I needed to broaden my horizons. I still missed her though. One afternoon as I walked into a cafe I saw a help wanted sign on the front, I was running low on cash and figured maybe I could get a little work here to continue my trip.

The waitress passed me as I walked in, "just sit anywhere hun."

I decided to sit at the counter and find out about the job.

"What'll you have?" I ordered the country fried steak and asked about the job. "Hey Eddie, this guy wants to know about the job." He looked at me through the cooks window and told me it was just helping him cook and dishes mostly, but he would be out in a few and talk to me if I was interested. I nodded and after I was done eating he came out and sat next to me.

"We had a guy here for a while, but he got arrested the other night, so it is just me and Debby for the most part. I could use some help with the cooking and then of course clean up and dishes always have to be done. Have you ever done any cooking?"

"Well at home I did, but never in a restaurant."

"It's not hard, mostly you would have to run the deep fryer and prep food so I don't have to do it." I looked over to my other side and noticed Debby sitting there.

"Oh please say you can do it! I am soooo tired of doing everything around here!" She smiled at me and put her hands together as if she were praying, I laughed and said sure I would give it a try.

"Where you from kid?" Eddie asked me.

"I live a few hundred miles north of here and have just been traveling a bit for the last month."

"You plan on sticking around a while? I really don't want to hire someone for only a couple of days." I hadn't given much thought to that; I had slept in my car a few times, stayed with relatives or stayed at the Y for the most part.

"Hmmm.. I am not sure actually, I don't have a place to stay yet."

"Tell you what kid, there is a small apartment upstairs, I mostly use it for storage, but if you clean it up you can stay there until you find something else."

"Oh Eddie, that place is tiny and dirty." Debby explained.

"I don't mind, I am sure it will be an improvement over my back seat and if there is a shower it will be like the Ritz to me!"

"Before you say that I had better let you look at it." Eddie said with a grin.

"I can take him up Eddie, you wanna see it?" I told her sure and we walked through the kitchen and out the back. There was a pretty rickety looking set of stairs going up and I couldn't imagine a big guy like Eddie walking up them carrying supplies.

As we opened the door I could see she was right, it was small, full of cases of food and really dusty!

"See what I told you? Definitely not the Ritz!" I didn't care at this point, it would be my own space and I had never had that before. I turned to her and told her it would be fine, I just needed to clean it up a bit and move some of the food out of the way.

"Tell you what hun, we close tomorrow and I will give you a hand cleaning it up if you want."

"Oh no, you don't have to do that, I am sure you have better things to do."

"Yeah, I could clean my trailer instead.. woo hoo!" She laughed at me and made a silly face.

"I will make you a deal, you help me and I will help you."

"You don't have to do that, I don't mind at all." She replied. I told her it was that or nothing, and after a bit of coaxing she agreed.

"You know I have been on the road and by myself a lot, so it will be nice to have someone to talk to for a change." With that we walked out and back to the dining room.

"Well kid, what do you think? We got a deal?" I said sure, and he responded by throwing me an apron.

"Ok come on in, let me show you what needs to be done before the dinner rush, by the way what is your name?"

"Justus."

The rest of the day went by in a minute, and when I finally stopped to catch my breath Eddie looked over at me and started laughing.

"Kid you got more food on you than there is on the floor!" I looked down and realized I must have rubbed my hands on my apron about a thousand times; I looked like I was wearing half the food in the kitchen. Debby walked in and started to laugh at me too, and I suddenly felt silly and my face grew warm.

"Look at you! Oh my god, that is too funny! Are you blushing? You are just too cute." I felt like an idiot all of a sudden and only smiled and went back to the sink overflowing with dishes.

"Hey Justus, I didn't mean to embarrass you, I was just giving you a hard time."

"It's ok." I said as I started to wash the mountain of dishes in front of me.

"Tell you what, I will give you a hand as soon as I am done out front."

"You don't have to do that, I can handle it."

"I'm sure you can, but I have had to do this myself the last few nights and I know where everything goes." I hadn't thought of that and agreed I could use the help.

Much later the work was done and I was exhausted, I never knew it could be so hard to work in a kitchen, and thought of the days and nights my mom had cooked for me and my dad all those years. I missed her and wrote her every week, and of course I still missed Janice a lot.

"So what did you think Justus, you still want to work here?"

Debby grinned at me and made a hopeful look simultaneously.

"Not like I have a lot of choices, and besides I wouldn't want you to have to do this every night by yourself!" I laughed a fake laugh and pretended to flex my muscles. "My hero!" we both laughed for a minute and then looked at the now clean kitchen.

Eddie had finished about an hour earlier and left, so Debby and I walked out the back and she locked the door behind her.

"Let me give you a hand settling in if you would like."

"You don't have to do that."

She cut me off, "I know I don't have to, but you don't even know where the lights are!" She was right.

"Ok, let me get my stuff out of my car" We walked up the stairs with the light of the street shining on the back of the building. The cafe was in the middle of the block and there was a narrow road in back with enough room for me to park in and still allow cars to pass. "Ok Justus, the main light switch is behind the door for some reason, so it is a pain to find in the dark sometimes. Flicking it on it cast a dim light through most of the room.

"There isn't much to it as you know, but over here behind all the cases is the bathroom, you can find the switch here by the sink." The bathroom was really pretty much in the main room, but all the cases of food acted like a wall to give a slight amount of privacy, not that I would need it.

"Thank you Debby, I am sure I will be fine."

"I have no doubt, anyone who drives all over the country alone must be very capable of taking care of himself, I admire your sense of adventure and wish I could do it." I started to ask her why she couldn't, but she cut me off and pointed at the bed.

"You might have to shake the dust off of it, but it is not too bad, I have slept up here a couple times when I didn't feel like driving home, usually after a few beers!" She winked at me and said she would be by in the morning to give me a hand. I thanked her again as she closed the door behind her.

The next day arrived too soon, and I was jarred awake by the sound of a knock on the door.

"Just a minute!" I looked at my watch, 7 am!? What the heck, who would be up here that early! I pulled my pants on and opened the door.

"Ooo, nice chest!" Debby said as she poked a finger into it. I felt embarrassed and just said "Debby, I didn't expect you so early!"

My face grew warm again as she spoke.

"I think it is sooo cute how you blush so easily!" She laughed and walked past me carrying a bucket, mop and cleaning supplies.

"Most guys don't even know what a blush is, let alone ever do it. Of course most guys are jerks." I couldn't argue with her, it seemed like most of the men I had known in my life were assholes, and with the exception of the sheriff never met one I looked up to.

"How do you know I am not a jerk?" I asked as I pulled my shirt on.

" I am not sure really, but you seem like a nice guy and from what you told me last night about your mom I can tell you love her, and miss her. Most guys wouldn't admit they missed their mom, it shows you are sensitive. Have you ever had a girlfriend?" I wasn't sure what to say and just stood there for a minute.

"I'm sorry, that is none of my business."

"No, it's ok, I don't really want to talk about her is all."

"I understand."

We spent the rest of the morning cleaning and moving cases of food around, she went down to the diner and brought some pie and milk up earlier, but I was starting to get hungry again.

"Are you getting hungry Debby? I could run down to the Mc Donald's and grab a couple burgers."

"Oh don't do that Justus."

"It's ok, I can afford it!" I smiled and pulled out a couple of wadded up dollars. "No it isn't that, but since they opened it has hurt our business and I hate them, a lot of local folks do too, and if you went in there while working here it would look bad."

"I hadn't thought of that, what do you want to do?"

"I don't want to spend any more time in the restaurant than I have to, but we are about done here, maybe we can go back to my place and I can make us something there." I looked around, it was much cleaner and since we moved all the food to one side it looked much bigger. I left a 'wall' of food cases by the bathroom in case anyone needed to use it they would have some privacy.

"Sure, now it's my time to help you!"

"I was just kidding Justus, you don't have to help me, it was nice to be able to give you hand."

"A deal is a deal, so lets go."

"Ok, but I drive!"

"My pleasure, I am happy to take some time off from behind the wheel!"

Pulling into the little trailer park where she lived she told me her place wasn't much, but at least it was hers. I started to ask her how come she didn't have a boyfriend or husband, but then thought of her question earlier and how it was probably none of my business this time. Inside the small trailer I found it to be spotless.

"I thought you said you needed to clean your place today also, this place is immaculate!"

"Ok, I lied, I have no life and when I am here seems like all I do is clean."

I now was really curious, she was about mid 20's I thought, she had a really cute face, long brown hair and brown eyes, she wasn't thin like Janice, but not fat either. I thought of her as being strong and the way she helped me move the cases of food I could see I had been right.

"I think you have done enough cleaning for one day anyway, so let me make you a sandwich or something instead. Would you like a beer?"

"Uh, I am not 21."

"Really?! I thought you must be, I am surprised! Well anyway I'm not going to call the cops or anything." She winked at me and I said sure, I wouldn't mind a beer.

We spent the rest of the day talking and she drove me around the little town. There were a few factories and she explained this was probably the only reason the town even existed.

"You will notice that we are dead while the guys are at work, but we can always count on the lunch and dinner rush."

"So is that why you don't open on Sunday?"

"Yep, no one comes in anymore from the highway, now that the damn McDonalds is there." We pulled up behind the cafe as it was getting dark.

"I really enjoyed spending the day with you Justus, you are a great guy and I like your company."

"I had a great day too, it was nice to not be alone, and to get to know you better."

"Be ready tomorrow for work, we open at 7."

"Oh crap, I don't have an alarm clock...."

"I will come up and bang on your door then, ok?"

"Thanks, I will get one after work tomorrow."

Before I knew it there was a knock on the door.

"Justus, you up?" I looked at my watch, it was 6:30.

"Uhhh... yeah I am."

"Ok, hurry down if you want to get something to eat before we open." I heard her walk back down the steps and in a few minutes I was also back in the cafe.

Over the next week I worked most of the daylight hours and grew to respect Debby a great deal, not only did she work like a maniac, but she tolerated all the crap she got from the guys that would come in. I started to get annoyed by the way they would smack her on the butt anytime she turned to walk away, along with all the stupid jokes and innuendo. I began to understand why she was single in this little town. I would soon find out the real reason.

AN UNEXPECTED TURN

I found as my respect grew for Debby so did my admiration. She always seemed to be in a good mood even when things were difficult at the job. I started to think of her more and Janice less.

One night after a really long day she came into the kitchen,

"Justus, what do you say I grab us a couple beers while we finish up in here?"

"Sure why not, a beer would taste good right about now."

Going out the back door she told me she would be back in a second. I was working fast trying to get everything done so I could sit down and enjoy a beer with her, about then she came back in with a 12 pack in her hand.

"I thought you said a couple of beers!"

"This is a couple of beers around here!" Laughing she opened the pack and popped one open for me.

"Do you think Eddie will get mad if I drink on the job?"

"You are so funny! No, it's not like we are getting drunk or anything, and he pretty much lets me do what I want." I thought about how hard it would be for him to replace her and that he probably would have a difficult time finding anyone that worked as hard as she did.

"Let me help you finish up, and we can get outta here. "With her help we had everything done before we finished our second beer.

"Come on Justus, let's lock up and go upstairs and take a load off our feet." I was more than happy to get off my feet, after not standing for long periods while traveling they were plenty tired at the end of the day. We sat down on the edge of my bed and started to talk about my travels and about how she hadn't been anywhere for a long time.

"You are young still, I am sure you will do a lot of traveling someday." I assured her.

"I doubt it, I would love to get out of this town, but by myself... I don't know if I could do that. And I am not as young as you, it's easy to get baggage very quickly."

"How old are you Debby." She gave me a funny look and said that guys shouldn't ask a girl how old she was, then smiled and said "26, although most days I feel 46!" I laughed at her and told her she sure didn't look 46!" Giving me a hug she smiled and asked if I wanted another beer.

"Sure I guess, but I think I am getting a buzz, and I gotta pee!" I got up and started to the toilet as she cracked open a couple more beers.

"Yep, definitely feeling the beers!" I said as I walked awkwardly across the room.

"Justus you are so cute! Hey does this radio work?"

" I haven't tried it actually, usually I just fall straight to sleep." I heard some static as I started to pee, and thought it was better than her hearing me go, and how odd it was that there was a woman only a few feet from me. In a couple seconds she had a good station and I walked back to where she was still sitting.

Handing me the beer she told me how nice it was to be able to spend time with me, and how it had been a while since she had felt like she had a friend. "Of course I am your friend, and you are really the only friend I have as well." Unexpectedly she leaned over and kissed me. I didn't know what to do and for a moment just sat there like someone who had never kissed anyone. She pulled back "Oh Justus, I am sorry, I shouldn't have done that."

"No, it's ok, I just didn't expect it."

"That's good, I wouldn't want to gross you out or anything!"

"You don't have to worry about that, I think you are really cute."

She smiled and gave me a big hug holding me close enough that I could feel her heartbeat.

"Justus, you are so sweet, no one has told me I am cute for a long time. Most of the stupid guys just say crap like 'hey sexy" or " hot stuff" lame things like that and I know all they want is to get in my pants."

"Well they are jerks and you should ignore them, I have seen them smack your butt and other stuff sometimes, if I were you I would punch them!"

"You know I can't do that, I don't want someone getting mad and causing trouble for me, besides I need their tips, unfortunately." We had a couple more beers as we talked and listened to the radio, I was feeling pretty lightheaded and told her I needed to get cleaned up before I couldn't stand up!

"Do you mind if I just sit here and listen to the music while you do? We don't have to work tomorrow and going home to an empty house is just depressing." I felt a little awkward having her there while I got undressed, but with the food cases stacked up you couldn't see anything so I told her I didn't mind, even though I was really self conscious. As I undressed she continued to talk to me and thanked me for letting her hang out.

"Hey, you bought the beers, I couldn't just throw you out!" We chuckled at this and she said 'yeah there were still a couple left that needed to be drank!

The hot water felt good on my face, and the buzz I had made me feel warm head to toe.

"Well as soon as I get out of here I will have to help you finish them off!" I kinda laughed and then almost fell over when I heard her reply.

"After your shower we can" She was right behind me and as I spun around she stood there naked in front of me. I didn't know what to say or do and just stood there for what seemed like an eternity.

"I hope you don't mind, I was feeling a bit dirty too."

The way she said it made the water seem all of a sudden much hotter.

"Justus, you are blushing again, that is so cute!" She started to get in and I managed to say it was ok, she had just surprised me. Pushing up against me in the small shower, she asked, "Was it a good surprise?" She put her arms around me and I could feel myself getting aroused, I hadn't felt this since Janice and was embarrassed.

"Never mind Justus, I know your answer."

With that she looked in my eyes and once again kissed me. I hadn't really thought of ever being with anyone since Janice had left me, but now here I was with Debby. She felt so soft and warm to me and as we continued to kiss the memories of the passion I had felt before came back. We stumbled from the shower and to the bed without even drying off, and over the next couple hours became as one it seemed. She was so intuitive and I felt like she knew everything I was thinking. We made love until it was very late and then fell asleep in each other's arms.

"Justus, are you awake?" I opened my eyes to see Debby looking at me with a smile on her face. Before I could speak she continued, "I hope you are ok with what happened last night. I don't want you to think I am a tramp, and that I do this sort of thing with just anybody." I have really only been with one guy for a long time but you are so kind to me and treat me like I matter, I just wanted you to know how much I appreciate it and how much I care about you."

"Debby, of course I am ok with us being together, you are one of the nicest women I have ever known, and I wouldn't change anything." She pulled me close and I put my arm around her. I was all of a sudden aware of the feelings I was having for her, and didn't want that to happen. I remembered how much it hurt when Janice had left and never wanted to feel that again, and how I was really just passing through here, I was going to continue to travel....what was happening? I decided to tell her about Janice.

"Debby, remember how you asked me about if I had ever had a girlfriend?" I proceeded to tell her all about Janice but of course left out the parts about what I had done to her husband.

"Wow Justus, you were actually with a married woman? And here I thought you were so innocent!" She grinned and said it was funny how ironic life can be.

"I wish I was still young and innocent, it seems time goes by so fast and things happen that you never expect. I didn't expect to ever be with someone that was so sweet and caring and I don't regret being with you either."

We got up a little while later and she asked me to come back to her place and she would make me breakfast. The next few days went by quickly and we of course worked every night as we had before, only now she would come up after and we would spend the evenings together. I found myself much more annoyed by the stupid men that would come in and flirt with her and touch her, but I knew there was nothing I could do about it.

One day later that week a man came in well before the dinner rush. As Debby walked from the kitchen she started "You can have a seat.." but stopped short and just froze up.

"I will sit back here as usual." He said in a low tone. She came back in the kitchen and I could see she was upset.

"Are you ok" I asked, she only nodded, turned to Eddie and nudged him. He looked out in the dining room and said he would watch. I couldn't figure out what was going on, and wondered if this guy might be a criminal or something. I continued washing the dishes knowing that Eddie was watching whatever was going on out there. Eddie walked behind me and said he needed to get some stuff from upstairs and for me to take care of any orders that might come in. I walked to the grill and could see Debby sitting down talking to this man. Why was she doing that? She never sat down and chatted with customers! I looked at her face as she spoke so quietly that I couldn't make out what she was saying. Her face had a look of someone that just found out their mom had died.

She started to shake her head no, but eventually dropped her eyes to the table and nodded 'ok'. My curiosity was killing me, I wanted to ask her right then what was going on, but as I contemplated this the man got up and walked out. Debby continued to sit there for a while, then glanced up noticing that I was looking at her. I thought I saw her wipe a tear and thought that maybe someone she loved had died. As she walked in the kitchen I asked her if everything was ok, nodding she said yes and I had better hurry up and finish cleaning before the dinner rush. I felt like she was blowing me off and for a minute got upset, then I had to remind myself that it was none of my business and she didn't owe me any explanation.

The rest of the day I was frustrated, why wouldn't she talk to me? I started to think I had made a big mistake allowing myself to have such strong feelings for someone I hardly knew, but it was too late, I cared about her so much and thought she felt the same way up 'til now.

The last customer left the cafe and she locked the front door. As usual I had a big mess to clean and hoped maybe Debby would tell me what was going on as we cleaned up. Instead after she had all her work done she came to me. "Justus, I am not going to be able to help you finish tonight, so you will have to lock up." As she handed me the keys I just stared at her.

"What's going on? What happened today, I have not seen you smile once since that guy left. Is everything ok?"

"I am fine, it's nothing, please make sure and lock up. I will try and stop by later if I can." Her words trailed off and she walked out the back. This was too much! I had to find out what was going on. I looked out the back door and saw her walking the opposite way of where her car was parked. I decided I needed to follow her and locked the door behind me. I quickly got within sight of her, but made sure she didn't see me. There was nothing around here but houses and I couldn't understand why she hadn't driven. I noticed a semi parked on the street and to my surprise she was heading straight to it. I stopped in my tracks.

What the hell?? She was getting into the truck! I decided I was going to get closer and see if I could hear anything. I could only hear muffled voices coming from the sleeper and wondered what was being said. My insides were shaking and for a minute I thought I would be sick, but as I thought of this I realized the talking had stopped. I imagined what was happening in there, her now kissing him, and who knew what else. I turned and ran as fast as I could back to my room. I unlocked the door and was suddenly aware of tears in my eyes. Damn it! Why did I allow myself to get feelings for her?? I tried to put it out of my mind but screamed out loud instead "how could you go to him!!" I felt like exploding and threw myself on my bed. I thought about how shortly before she was here in this bed with me, and now... I didn't want to think of it.

I was up for a while my mind torturing me as to why I had allowed myself to feel anything for anyone again. Instead of just staying there and wallowing in self-pity, I forced myself to get up and go finish my work.

My sleep was fitful and the next morning I had to fight to get out of bed. "Hey kid, you look like crap, what'd you do, stay up all night partying?" I laughed it off and told him I wasn't feeling good was all. While we talked and prepped food Debby came in.

"You're running a bit behind today Debby, what, did you and Justus both go to the same party?" He laughed as he walked past me and I looked through the window at Debby. She looked different, I noticed she was wearing makeup and wondered who she was trying to impress since she rarely had any on. All of a sudden as she came closer I could see something else, her face looked different, there was a bruise under that makeup, and even that wouldn't hide the swelling. Just then Eddie came back in. Looking at her he shook his head and muttered "oh Debby" Looking at me I could see the pain in her eyes as she turned and started to work. I was angry, hurt and confused. I had to talk to her, to find out what was happening.

The day seemed to drag on forever and as the last customer left I hoped she would stay and help me tonight. Eddie left and she was still working out front, she hadn't spoke to me all day and I wondered if she would now. I turned around to see her standing a few feet away looking at me.

"Justus, I need to talk to you. There is something you don't know." I looked at her and thought about what she was going to say next. I had an idea, but quietly sat there waiting. Her eyes filled with tears as she began to speak.

"Justus, I know you saw me with that man yesterday here in the restaurant...Justus,.....he is my husband.

I couldn't believe my ears! What in the world was going on here??!! A million thoughts went through my mind at that moment, why did I seem to fall for married women and how come the two women that I was with were not only married, but also mistreated?

I thought back to when Debby and I were talking and how she said it was "ironic" when I told her about Janice being married. I was hurt, confused, angry, and at the moment speechless as she looked at me and tried to hold back the tears. I didn't know what to say, I could see the pain in her eyes, and the mark on her face and for a minute felt her pain and knew what it was like to be a victim all over again. Her head dropped and she just looked at the floor. "Justus, I don't expect anything from you, you don't even have to talk to me if you don't want to. I didn't mean to hurt you."

"Then why did you go to him last night?"

"How did you know about that? You were working when I left." For a minute she looked angry, but then more ashamed.

"I'm sorry, I had no business following you, it was immature, but you know how much I like you, and I had to know what was going on."

"You have no idea at what you have gotten yourself into, he is on the road most of the time, but when he is here he expects me to be with him, if I refuse... well... Justus, I refused and you see what happened. Please don't hate me, I should have told you at the beginning, but I never imagined I could have such feelings for you."

I was still reeling from everything I had experienced in the last 12 hours but reached for her, she immediately put her arms around me as we held each other close.

"You are so much different than any man I have ever known, you don't look at me like a piece of meat, or a conquest. You really care... I am not used to that." I didn't say anything, but only pulled her tighter to me.

As we worked that night she told me about how she had met him a few years ago and how he had seemed so nice. After a while on the road things changed, he would accuse her of cheating on him with everyone in town. She never had but that didn't stop him from believing it. At first he would only yell at her and call her names like tramp and whore, but one night after he had been drinking he hit her, and it only got worse from there.

She had never been unfaithful to him but recently told him she wanted a divorce, all that did was get her beaten and he told her she would die before she left him. Eddie knew about it and had volunteered to 'speak' with him, but she knew that would only make things worse.

Now the rumors were going around that she was seeing someone. People had seen that her car wasn't home many nights lately and told him about it. "Justus, no one suspects it is you and you can leave this dead end town now and nobody will ever know. I don't want to see you get hurt."

"I am not afraid, and am not going to leave."

My mind went back to Janice once more and how she had tried to protect me, I didn't need protection anymore, I remembered the price my mom paid more than once for trying to protect me.

"I can take care of myself Debby, besides he doesn't know a thing."

"Not yet, but he will be back tomorrow tonight and if I don't meet him at the bar… well, something bad will happen."

"No, nothing will happen to you or to me." She looked at me and told me that no matter what she trusted me, and knew I wouldn't do anything to hurt her. That night after work she came upstairs with me.

"Justus no matter what else happens I want to stay with you tonight." She made love to me and held me close all night long as if she would never be able to again.

In the morning she told me that she would have to go to the bar that night, "If I don't I will be in trouble, and so might you."

"I am not afraid."

"You should be." with that she got dressed and we went downstairs.

About an hour after the lunch rush I spoke with Eddie.

"Debby told me about her husband."

"I am surprised kid, but I imagine you saw the bruise and she must have thought you would figure it out. I told her I would take care of it, but she won't have it."

"Why not?"

"He was in the military from what I understand, and has issues with violent behavior. I suppose she is afraid he would do something to me" I just nodded and turned back to my work.

I had already decided what I was going to do, and how. When Debby told me how he had said to her she would die before she left him, I knew he was not lying.

"Hey Eddie, I am not feeling very good, I think I need to go get something for my stomach."

"Ok, just hurry, the dinner crowd will be here soon." I went out the back and hoped Debby wouldn't know I had left. Running to the pharmacy across the street I spoke to the pharmacist.

"My aunt sent me to get some sleeping pills for her, but I am not sure what to get."

"Well son, a lot of folks like these" he told me as we walked over to where there were a number of choices. "They are fairly strong and don't have a lot of side effects." He continued.

"How many should she take?"

"The directions are inside, but usually one or two will take care of the problem."

"Thank you, I appreciate your help." I paid and ran back to work.

The dinner rush came and went.

"Eddie, I am still feeling really sick, I am not sure I am going to be able to finish my work."

"What's wrong kid, your stomach still bothering you? Don't be telling anyone that, they might think you got it here from my food!" He laughed for a second, but then continued "I need this cleaned up you know."

"I will get up early if I have to, but I really feel terrible."

"Debby, come here, hey Justus is sick. Can you clean up for him?" She looked at me for a minute and then said " hang on, I will let you know." Motioning to me to come to her I walked out to the dining room.

"Justus, you know I have to meet my husband tonight, are you faking this?"

"Of course not, maybe it is just all the stress, but I am really sick."

"Ok, I will call the bar and tell them to give him the message that I will be late, but I HAVE to go, please understand."

"I do, and appreciate you helping me out."

"Justus, I would do anything for you."

"Thank you, and know that I will make it up to you."

I felt strange as I walked out the back and headed to the bar. It was as if I was going back into the deep woods, nobody could see what I was thinking or doing, like walking into a dark room where only you could see. The day my dad died my pain did as well. Anytime I felt that pain all I could think of was him and I would do whatever it took to alleviate it.

The bar was small and smelled of cigarettes, I hated that stench, it reminded me of the man that called me his father. This would not be hard I knew. I had seen the semi in back of the cafe and knew he would be there. For the first time in my life something my dad had taught me was going to be useful. I had been to the bar with him a lot when I was younger, I think he had hoped to make me more like him, but of course this was not going to happen. Regardless I had learned to play pool, now I would make use of that skill.

Seeing her worthless husband playing at the back table I watched for a minute.

"You are pretty good, like a challenge?"

He sneered at me, "from you?"

"Sure, how about loser buys the drinks."

"Ok punk, you got a game." I lost the first game on purpose and went to get the beers. For once I was glad to not get asked for my ID. The bartender gave them to me and already having a couple pills in my hand, put them in his beer. "Well you beat me that one, but I want a rematch!"

"Sure punk, I love free beers!" I hated this guy already so much but smiled and racked the balls. I lost the next one as well and repeated my steps; I could see him getting groggy and now decided to win.

"You little bastard, I should have won that game!" He exclaimed as I sunk the eight ball.

"I'll tell you what, you give me the money and I will even go and get the next round!" He handed me a couple bucks and off I went. It was starting to get late and I became concerned that Debby would walk in and see me here playing pool with him. Twenty minutes later he was visibly drunk and in a stupor from the pills.

"Hey buddy, you up for another game?" Looking at me with glazed over eyes he said, "I think I need to lay down for a minute."

"Is that your rig behind the cafe?" He nodded and I said I was heading back that way and needed to go as well. He staggered back and I hoped Debby wouldn't intercept us. The cafe was dark and I wondered where she was, I figured she must have went home to clean up and change and that thought made me more determined than ever to finish what I had started.

"That's a hell of a rig" I said as we drew closer, " can I see inside of it?"

"Sure, yeah whatever" he mumbled as he climbed up into the truck. Falling into the back part, he grunted something about 'where was that bitch' and in a minute I heard him snoring. I quickly looked around and saw there wasn't much here I could use. I peeked in back and couldn't see anything in the dark. I decided I needed a flashlight and something else. I got out of the cab and ran up to my room where I had seen a flashlight. Getting back into the cab I shone the light where he was passed out.

Hmmm.. a half pack of cigarettes, a couple bottles of booze, some men's magazines and a pile of dirty clothes. Nice I thought, just what every 'real man' needs.

My thoughts again returned to my dad and what he thought was a real man.

I looked at the pack of cigarettes and chuckled as I said out loud "didn't you know that cigarettes can be hazardous to your health?" I already knew that fire cleaned up evidence and this was too easy.

"Enjoy Hell, tell Bob I said hello."

Pouring some liquor on the clothes and magazines, I lit the cigarette, dropped the match and got out. I walked up the stairs and into my room where I waited for the fire trucks.

I was amazed that it took so long for the fire to be visible, but when one of the windows broke, it took off and was soon engulfing the semi. I waited for an explosion and worried that it might start the cafe and my room on fire, but it never happened.

Even after the fire was visible it took the fire department close to fifteen minutes to get there, by then there was not much left inside I was sure. I heard the sirens and pretended to be surprised at what was going on. Eddie and Debby showed up soon after the trucks got there.

"Hey kid, did you see what happened?"

"No Eddie I was asleep."

"Wow, there is not much left of that truck!"

Debby just looked at the truck and at me, she knew it was his truck, but she only stood there and stared.

"Captain!, we have a fatality here!" A fireman jumped from the smoldering cab and the fire chief made his way to the truck. I couldn't hear them talk, but shortly the chief walked over to Debby.

"Hey Debby, everyone in this town knows this is your husbands truck, as well as you...and now you know he is dead." He was so matter-of-fact, and for some reason it didn't surprise me. Debby again looked at me and then back at the fire chief

"I know, but thank you for telling me." I knew what small town life was like and therefore realized a lot of people had an idea of what was going on.

"Debby, are you ok?" I didn't know what to say and this seemed like a stupid, question but had to ask it. "Yes, I am fine why would I care?" Her honesty surprised me and I admired her for it.

The night was a mess of trucks, cars, and people milling around just for the sake of curiosity. I went back upstairs when I saw Debby talking to the sheriff, I didn't want to answer any questions.

The next day I awoke to the sound of a knock.

"Is your name Justus Walken?" It was the sheriff and I just nodded as if still asleep, but was immediately awake.

"Sorry to bother you, but Eddie said you needed to be up anyway." He kinda smiled and continued. "Did you see anything last night?"

"Not until I heard the sirens, I was sick and left work early."

"Yeah, Eddie said that, but some people saw you at the bar." I wasn't ready for this, and hadn't thought about what to do in case this happened.

"Oh yes, I did go over there actually, I didn't tell Eddie, but my dad died 2 years ago yesterday and I was upset. He and I used to play pool together so I went over there to play a couple games."

"I am sorry to hear that, did you know the man you were playing pool with?"

"Not really, but he left about the same time as me, and I just came home here." I was sweating profusely and tried to keep my arms folded tightly so he couldn't see me shake.

"Ok son, we have to do some follow up work, and I needed to talk to you. Are you planning on being here for a while?"

"Yeah, I guess, I told Eddie I would work for him until he could find someone permanently."

"Alright, I will be in touch if I need anything else." He walked down the steps as I closed the door. My hands wouldn't stop shaking and my whole body was in a knot. I had never been questioned before and realized how careless I had been. If anyone had seen me get into that truck I could have been arrested. I finished getting dressed and walked down to work.

"Wow kid, what a night! Who'd have thought that could happen right in back? It will surely be the topic of conversation today!" He stopped short as Debby walked in.

"Morning sweetie, how you feelin' today?" He had a bit of a serious look on his face at that moment and she looked straight at him.

"Never better." He looked at me with half a smile and went back to work.

The day went by fast and he was right, everyone was talking about the fire, I could see some customers hug her, others would pat her on the back and say things like, "you are going to be fine" or, " you are better off." I had the feeling that a lot of people knew and was somewhat hurt that she had never said anything to me until she was in a corner.

The day passed, as they all do, and soon Debby and I were cleaning up. "Justus, I was wondering if it would be ok if I grabbed a few beers and came up tonight?" I thought it was odd that she asked, but told her of course it was fine and I always wanted to spend time with her. I finished up the work as she went to the store and soon we were up sitting on the edge of my bed. We cracked open a couple beers and I wasn't sure what to say, but finally managed to speak.

"Debby, I am sure you are not sad, but I just wanted you to know that I will be here for you if you need me.

" She stared deep into my eyes and then my heart stopped as she spoke. "Justus, I saw you get out of the truck last night, and I know what you did."

HONESTY

I felt all the blood drain from my face, and wasn't sure what to say right now, but before I could speak she did.

"You look pale Justus"

I cut her off, "Debby what are you talking about? I was sick last night, up here."

"Please don't lie to me, I think you are better than that." I didn't know how she could have possibly seen me and as I thought about this she continued. "Last night after work I was worried about you and came up to see how you were feeling, I knocked but you didn't answer so I let myself in to check and make sure everything was alright. When I found you were not here I started to leave but heard your voice and my husbands below. I saw you, get into the truck and was about to leave when you got back out. I hid in the shower and was going to surprise you if you saw me and then see what was going on. You came in and grabbed the flashlight and went back out." I tried to think of a good reason for all of this and argue, but she kept speaking. "I went back to the door and looked out as you got back into the cab. I wanted to know what was going on, but I was scared and decided to hide by the dumpster and see if I could hear anything. A few minutes later you got back out and went upstairs. I felt like running up behind you and ask you why you would have been in the truck, and what you could have been talking about, instead I just sat there and cried. Not too long after that I heard the window on the truck break and saw the fire, I decided to get out of there before the cops showed up."

"Debby, I am not sure what to say, I"

"Justus," she interrupted, " I want to show you something." With those words she reached into her purse and pulled out a gun.

"Holy crap Debby! What are you doing with that?!"

"When I was with him the other night it was to say that I would never be with him again, he hit me in the face and told me I was always going to be his whenever he wanted me. I jumped out of the truck and since he was already undressed he didn't try to chase me, but yelled at me that I had better meet him at the bar, or I would pay for it."

My heart sank as I thought of myself standing outside of the truck that night thinking she was giving herself to him.

She continued "I knew that if I went to him he would just rape me once more, and probably worse, I would rather die than be with him again. I decided that I would kill him before I would let him touch me. Justus, I love you, and you are the only one I want to ever touch me." I sat stunned at everything I was hearing and looking at the gun I knew she was serious.

"Debby, I don't know what to say, my feelings for you are very strong and I never wanted to feel like this again. After Janice I was hurt so bad I wanted to die and that is why I decided to take this trip, to just drive and never get attached to anyone again."

"I will never hurt you Justus, I hope you know that." I could see in her eyes that she meant it and I put my arms around her and as she hugged me back she whispered, "If you hadn't done it, I would have." I pulled back and looked at her and spoke.

"Why do you think I killed him? Don't you think it could have been an accident?"

"What other reason could you have for being there? I know you wouldn't have hung out with him because he was such a great guy, so what then? No matter what I will protect you, you can trust me."

I knew that I could and told her everything, she only nodded and said how brilliant I was and that there was no way they could ever figure out the truth. We spent the night together once again and I felt happy and content for the first time in a while. I knew she loved me and would never tell anyone what I had done, it was the first time I felt secure in a while.

The morning quiet was broken by a knock on my door. I pulled my pants on and opened it to see the sheriff standing there. I wondered why cops always came in the morning, maybe they hoped that I would be groggy and not remember my story from before.

"Morning Justus, I had a couple more questions I needed to ask you." He started again with why I had been at the bar when I was supposed to be sick, and how some people had seen me leave with Debby's husband.

"He wasn't feeling well so I helped him get back to his rig, I think he was just really drunk."

"Did anyone see you come back upstairs?"

"Umm, no... but he just got in his truck and I went to bed."

"I hate to tell you this son, but the fire chief thinks there might have been some foul play, he was not exactly liked around here and we have to figure out what happened." Just then Debby came up behind me.

"Justus honey, you don't have to protect me anymore, it's ok. Sheriff, I have been with Justus and saw him help my ex into the truck, he then came back up here and we were together all night." I turned to her and tried not to act surprised.

"Debby, I wasn't aware you were getting divorced." The sheriff said.

"I have all the papers at home and was just waiting for his signature."

"Is this true Justus?"

"Yes sir, it is." I decided to not say anything more if he continued to question me, but instead he only said to have a good day and thanks for the information. I closed the door and before I could speak she did, "see honey, I will do anything for you, just like what you have done for me." With a huge smile she hugged me, then said we had better get to work before we got fired!

I soon found out that once the sheriff knew something, so did the whole town! Most people said they were happy for her, some thought she was robbing the cradle, and the majority of the men didn't like it at all. Now if they flirted with her or touched her in any way, she would put them in their place. Eddie wasn't sure it was good for business, but he stood behind her. Rumors went around that her husband was killed, and although they didn't care for him, they wanted to know the truth. I noticed that the factory crowd seemed to be less and less as the time went by, Debby blamed it on Mc Donald's, but I had a feeling the rumors were starting to take their toll on business.

I had been in town now for a couple months, and my mom liked it because she could now write me letters as well as receive them. I moved in with Debby about a week after the death of her husband and we were both very happy. I wanted to start traveling again and one night brought it up.

"Debby, what do you think about going on the road with me?"

"Funny you should bring that up, I was thinking last night about how you came here and the plans you had before you met me. Lately the cafe has been very slow, and tips are not worth a crap."

"I noticed that too, I have told you more than once I want to pay my share around here."

" I know you do, I wanted you to save up your money so you could continue your journey, but I have to admit I was hoping you would want me to go with you." A slight smile appeared on her lips, and as she saw mine it broadened.

"I don't know if you know this yet Debby, but I couldn't leave here without you." She hugged me as I continued, "there is something I haven't told you yet, maybe you already know, but I love you."

" I had hoped that one day you would tell me that, I have purposely not said 'I love you' lately because I didn't want you to feel like you had to say it back. You of course know that I love you more than anyone or anything. There is something though that you don't know." I wasn't sure what to think and wondered what was coming next. "I had a life insurance policy on my ex, well actually he wasn't my ex yet, but you know what I mean. Anyway since his death was ruled an accident and he was in his truck I got a check last week." She got up and went into the bedroom returning a moment later with an envelope.

"Take a look." I opened it and pulled out the check...fifty thousand dollars!!

"Oh my god Debby, you are rich!"

"Well I wouldn't say rich, but WE are not going to have to worry about money for a while, and I want to see the country with you." I was stunned and kept looking at the check, I had never seen one so big and to me it was a million dollars.

"Debby, I am not sure what to say, but this is your money, not mine."

"If it wasn't for you Justus, I wouldn't have it, I would be dead or in prison right now. You gave me life and love and I want you to have everything I have, and everything I am. I love you more than I thought I could love anyone, without you I don't know what I would do."

Once again I was speechless, here I was with a woman that I loved, she wanted to travel with me and now we could go anywhere.

"What are we gonna tell Eddie?"

"I will talk to him, I have been there for a long time and he is like a big brother to me, he will understand."

The next day she pulled Eddie aside and told him about our plans, he hugged her and looked me straight in the eye, "if you ever do anything to hurt her, I will not be happy." Giving me a menacing look I knew he was serious.

"I would never do anything like that, I hope you believe me." He smiled and shook my hand.

"Kid, I do, maybe you are not such a 'kid' after all." We told him we would stay until he could find replacements, and he thanked us as we got back to work.

A week later as we loaded our things in my car, Eddie was there.

"I hope you two take care of each other and have a wonderful adventure!"

"Thank you Eddie, you will always be like the big brother I never had, Justus and I will keep in touch and I hope to see you again and tell you of all the great places we have been." We waved goodbye and started out on the adventure that would change our lives.

DISTURBING NEWS

I looked over at Debby and smiled as we started out on this adventure together. I couldn't remember when I looked at the future with so much optimism and a sense of a brand new beginning with someone else. I had saved up some of my own money and tried to pay for everything from food to gas, but she never would let me.

"If it wasn't for you I wouldn't be here with you now and the happiest I have ever been." She would tell me.

It was nice to be able to sleep in a hotel instead of my car, and our nights together seemed to get better with each passing day. Her passion for me and mine in return would make time fly by and many times we would make love until the early morning hours. I still thought of Janice from time to time and wondered how she was, but for the most part she was becoming a distant memory. There were few times that I thought of any of the lives I had taken, and when I did it was as if I could see it as one views a movie, I just watched someone do those things and therefore could separate myself from the deed.

I talked with my mom from time to time and wrote her postcards from wherever we happened to be. Debby kept asking me when she would be able to meet her, and I also wanted this.

One day about 6 months after I had left home I called my mom.

"Hello mom, how are things there?"

"Hi Justus, this is your aunt Linda."

"Oh hello, how have you been?" I was not expecting anyone but mom to answer the phone and instantly got a strange feeling.

"I have been fine Justus, how has your trip been?"

" Wonderful, did mom tell you about Debby?"

"Yes she did, but I need to talk to you about your mom." Her tone changed and I asked what was wrong.

"Justus, she has been sick for a little while now, and I am here to help her out.

Where are you?" I explained that we were maybe 1,000 or so miles from home, "I think you should come back home for a bit Justus, is that possible?" I told her of course I would right away and hung up the phone.

"Debby, you have been wanting to meet my mom, I guess now is the time." I told her about the conversation and she agreed we head back at once.

Two days later we were there. I looked around and noticed my moms flowers didn't look as good as they usually do, and the yard looked a bit unkempt.

"Mom, we are back, are you here?" Debby followed me into the house and suddenly my aunt appeared from around the corner.

"Crap Linda, you startled me!"

"I am sorry Justus, I didn't mean to. Your mom isn't here right now," she hesitated for a moment and then began again, "she stayed overnight in the hospital so they could do some tests."

"They don't even know what is wrong with her? What has been going on here?"

"She has been feeling very tired for a while now she told me, and she has lost a lot of weight, that and the cough she has made me worry about her. I thought at first it was just because she had a flu bug or something, but for her to miss work and not take care of her flowers is not like her."

"Ok, lets go to the hospital now then." Linda nodded and we all headed out.

Debby held my hand as we drove and told me everything would be fine. I was glad to have her here with me now and squeezed her hand.

"Hello sir, may I help you?"

"Yes I am here to see my mom, Mrs. Walken."

"Oh yes, she is in room 143 just down the hall to your right." Linda said she would wait there in the lobby, and Debby and I walked quietly down the hall. We entered the room and I could see a woman lying there sleeping. At first I didn't recognize her, my aunt hadn't told me how much weight she had lost! Mom had never been a thin woman and this woman was almost gaunt, her breathing seemed to be labored as she slept. I didn't want to wake her, but wanted to hug her so much at that moment. I let go of Debby's hand and walked to the edge of the bed.

"Mom," I put my hand on her arm, "I am home."

Slowly her eyes opened and I could see the sparkle as she smiled up at me. " Oh Justus, I have missed you so much!" She reached up and put her arms around me and I leaned down and hugged her close.

"Mom, this is Debby."

"Come here Debby and give me a hug too." Debby came over and mom pulled her in and told her how nice it was to meet the woman that made her son so happy. I thought Debby was going to cry as she turned back to me, and then she smiled broadly.

We stayed there and talked for a bit until I remembered Linda was waiting out front.

"I will go get her," Debby volunteered "and give you two a minute to chat."

"Mom, what happened? You never told me you weren't feeling well, you know I would have come home right away if you needed me."

"I know dear, but you were having a great adventure and for me it was like I was there with you every time you told me where you were and what you were doing. Besides I have had the flu before and can take care of myself."

"Yes I know that, but this is obviously not just the flu, you have lost so much weight."

"Yes I know, isn't it nice? I am finally skinny!" She laughed a bit but started to cough.

"What is wrong? Mom tell me the truth." She looked at me and the sparkle faded from her eyes, "son I have lung cancer." My eyes filled with tears and I tried to choke it back.

"Oh honey, don't cry, it will be ok." A warm tear ran down my face as I put my arms around her.

"Are they sure? How could you have lung cancer, you never smoked. Maybe they are wrong," I wanted to make it all better, to make it just go away.

"I have asked these questions too, but it is true. Even though I never smoked your father did, and it is called 'second hand smoke' apparently it is even worse than if I had smoked." My sorrow turned to anger now, that bastard chain smoked for years, now he was attacking my mom again, this time from beyond the grave. My hatred for him flared and I wished I could kill him all over again. Instead I comforted my mom and asked what could be done.

"They have treatments and I will start them tomorrow, in a few days I will be able to go home and then just come in for the treatments."

"That's good, I know everything will be fine, science and medicine has gotten a lot better than it was years ago and I know they will fix you right up." I had to stay positive and reassure her now, I knew she was scared and I had to be brave.

"Justus, I hope you won't be too embarrassed to claim me as your mom." I had no idea what she was talking about and started to protest.

"I am going to be a skinny bald woman! Part of the treatment will cause my hair to fall out, so I guess you might want to hide me at the house!" She laughed just a little and I smiled back at her.

"I am never ashamed of being seen with you, maybe I will shave my head too! Debby and I will do whatever needs to be done around the house to take care of you. Just then Debby and Linda came back in. I told Debby what was going on and she agreed, "Yes of course Mrs. Walken we can take care of whatever you need." I knew she meant it as she put her arm around me.

A few days later mom was back home, Linda went back to her house and it was just the three of us. Debby took care of moms flowers and did a lot of the cooking, I had flashbacks now and then about how it was when Janice was there, but now Debby and I didn't have to hide that we loved each other. One night as we ate dinner mom spoke.

"You two seem so happy together, it is wonderful to see. Have you ever thought of getting married?" I about choked and looked at her.

"What? That was out of the blue!"

"Well Justus you know that marriage is a good thing with the right people, and God would like it too."

Mom hadn't gone to church in years, but I knew she was religious and believed in God. I always had my doubts, if God was real how come so many good people were tortured by sadistic bastards? How come it always seemed like the good were used by the bad? I thought the idea of heaven and hell seemed like fairytales created by preachers to make you donate money to them. I decided a long time ago that the only one that could take care of those I cared about was me. Instead of saying anything that could upset her I just replied that maybe someday we would. Debby gave me a funny look that bordered on surprise and contentment.

The days passed and mom seemed to be in better spirits, her treatments made her sick sometimes but she said she was feeling better. Her hair did start to fall out and I told Debby I wanted to shave my head as a sign of support. To my surprise she said she thought that was a nice idea and she would help me do it. After it was all done she stood back and looked at me.

"You know what? I think I like it, you look pretty good, for a cue ball that is!" She pretended to polish my head, laughed and ran out of the bathroom and up the stairs to our room. I chased her and tackled her on the bed, looking up at me she pulled me close and kissed me softly.

"Your mom won't be back for a while, " I stopped her words with a kiss and slowly began to undress her.

All of a sudden I heard a car pull into the driveway and looked outside.

"Oh my god,"

"What is it Justus?" I didn't know what to say, but looked back at her, "it's Janice."

She began to get dressed and didn't say anything back to me.

"What's wrong Debby?"

"You told me all about her of course, but right now you seem upset by her being here. If you are over her, why do you care if she is here?" I didn't know what to say to this, she was right, why was I so upset by this? I had no idea but my stomach was full of butterflies and I didn't know how to act or what to do next. "Of course I am over her, I love you! I guess I just never thought she would be back around here." My words sounded feeble at best to me, but I had to try and reassure her.

"Well then, lets go down and say hello." She had a bit of a determined look on her face and took my hand tightly into hers. Before we were at the bottom of the stairs I heard a knock, and then the squeaking of the hinges as the door opened.

"Hello, is anyone here?"

"Hello Janice." My face suddenly felt like it was on fire and I didn't want Debby to see me.

Janice looked different than the day she left me, she had nice clothes on, and makeup, her hair was styled differently as well. As I looked at her I remembered why I had fallen for her in the first place, but now felt ashamed for thinking this with the woman that I loved holding my hand.

"This is Debby, Janice." She continued to hold my hand but reached out to shake hands with her other one and said "I am Justus' girlfriend."

"Oh, well hello, I am Janice, a friend of Justus' mothers."

"Yes, I know who you are." I had never seen Debby be so matter-of-fact that bordered on rude.

"Anyway," Janice continued, "I heard about your mom being ill and I wanted to come see how she was doing." She now spoke to me as if Debby had left the room, almost to the extent of snubbing her. I was suddenly aware that Debby had gripped my hand so hard that it almost hurt. I pulled away from her unintentionally but she responded to this by putting her arm around me.

"Wow Justus, when did you shave your head?!"

"Actually Debby just got finished doing it, since my mom is losing her hair I wanted to support her. I am going to keep it this way until she is better."

"That is sooo sweet! You are such a great guy, and if you don't mind me saying it looks really sexy on you!" Now I could tell she was trying to piss Debby off and decided it was time to end this little catfight.

"Mom will be at the hospital for a couple of hours Janice, I think she would love it if you surprised her by going to see her." Glancing at Debby then back to me she agreed and started toward the door.

"Well you two have fun, I will see you later Justus." She looked straight at me with the last part as she walked out and made sure Debby saw the look.

"What a bitch! How could you ever have been with her?" I decided to put this fire out quickly.

"I was just naive and innocent I guess." Nudging my ribs she commented how I wasn't so innocent anymore. Understatement of the year I thought as she started to pull me back upstairs. No Debby, someone else might show up.

"Ok, fine if you don't want me I have things to do outside." I started to protest, but she just walked out.

I hadn't seen this side of her and wasn't sure I liked it. I guess jealousy is never a good thing, but I understood and went out to her.

"I am really sorry Debby, you know I love you, it has just been emotionally difficult for me since we got back here. A lot has happened and I hope you understand."

"Of course I do, I know how hard all this has been for you, but it is not easy for me to see the 'other woman' and to know that she had you before I did."

"I had to feel that too with your ex, remember?"

"Yes and you killed him, should I kill her so I can feel better?" I was a bit upset that she would say this to me, and told her.

"I thought we agreed that we wouldn't ever talk about that again, besides Janice didn't abuse me."

"Yes she did, she hurt you a lot, just not physically." I had to agree that I was hurt, but that she was trying to do what was right for me.

"Exactly Justus, so are you happy now? Is being with me the right thing?" I reassured her that it was, but still had to push the feelings for Janice down inside of me.

Later mom pulled back in the driveway followed by Janice.

"Justus honey, I am back." I thought it was cute the way she always announced herself as if we might be doing something she didn't want to know about.

"Hi mom, how was your day?"

"Typical except for Janice surprising me at the hospital, she said it was your idea. You are so sweet, I thought it would be nice if she stayed for dinner, just like the old days huh?" I could tell it made her happy so I agreed, Debby wasn't happy and let me know. I had a feeling this would be a strange night. I had no idea.

A CONFLICT

"Justus, I don't want to have dinner with your ex girlfriend! Just knowing you slept with her and she is here now makes me crazy."

"Debby, you know I don't have feelings for her anymore, and besides that my mom wants her here and it is her house."

I have to admit when I told her I didn't have feelings anymore for Janice it wasn't the complete truth. I don't know if anyone ever gets past their first love, and seeing her again definitely brought out feelings I thought were gone.

"I know it is your moms house, but if she knew the whole story I doubt she would feel the same way about her."

"Debby, I hope you would never even think of saying anything to her about Janice and I."

"Of course I wouldn't, I know it would hurt your mom and she is a good woman."

"Thank you for that." I put my arms around her and reassured her that she was the one that I loved and Janice would be leaving soon.

Dinner was a bit awkward and I could feel the tension between Debby and Janice. I assumed that Janice knew I had told Debby about the time we had spent together, but I couldn't get why she made a point of aiming comments at Debby that would upset her. If I didn't know better I would have thought she was jealous.

Finally dinner was over and soon Janice would be leaving.

"Janice, it is so nice to see you again, I have missed the time we used to spend together. I am looking forward to our morning coffee!"

"Betty you are so sweet, I have also missed that. I can stop by in the morning and visit for a while if you would like."

"Janice, don't be silly, you are staying here tonight." I froze at her words, and Debby just looked at me with surprise, then disgust as she walked upstairs. I wasn't sure what to say, but had to think of something since Janice just asked me what I thought of that idea. "It's ok with me, whatever mom wants." It was a weak reply at best and mom said it was settled then, she could sleep in her old room since it was the same as when she left.

"Like old times, huh Justus." Janice winked at me and I felt a rush of blood to my face, but turned quickly and mumbled something about 'more or less'. "Where are you going Justus, I was hoping we could all play a game or something." I realized that mom hadn't had so much company in a while and wanted to enjoy this evening.

"I am going to see if Debby is ok, then I will be right back." I walked in my room and was greeted by a glare.

"I don't want to sit around and play games with HER!"

"Please be nice Debby, it is only one night. She will be gone soon."

"I don't care, she is purposely trying to make me mad, everything she says is a dig. I hate that you had sex with her!"

"That is the past, I am with you now, that is what matters." She looked at me and her face softened.

"Ok Justus, I will put up with her for you and your mom." She hugged me and told me she loved me, then back downstairs we went.

"Now it's her turn," she mumbled as we got to the bottom, I started to ask her what that meant, but mom interrupted me. "How about a game of euchre?

Debby do you know that one?"

"Of course I do, doesn't everyone in the mid west know that one!?" They both laughed and I hoped the tension would be gone, but I had my doubts.

Debby and I played against mom and Janice, and now I knew what she had meant by 'now it's her turn'. Any chance she got there would be a comment aimed at Janice, but spoken to mom or me. If we won the hand maybe it would be "Justus and I are just the best team ever!" or "Justus is so in tune with me, like we are one person". She would offer to get mom or me a snack, or drink and snub Janice altogether. I really didn't like this kind of attitude and it made her seem less attractive to me.

"How about you Janice, is there anything you would like?" I decided that no matter what she was still a guest and I wouldn't allow this.

"Oh Justus, you are so kind to offer, a beer would be nice." Debby definitely didn't like this and I was sure she would tell me about it first chance she got.

She excused herself and went into the bathroom. I got Janice a beer and as I handed it to her she put a note in my hand. I started to look at it but she looked at my mom and then me shaking her head not to. I put it in my pocket just as Debby called me.

"Justus, could you come here for a minute?" Great, I knew what was coming next. I walked to the bathroom and she closed the door behind us.

"Why are you being so nice to her!"

"Because you are being so mean. I think it is uncalled for, you are better than that."

"I don't care, she is a bitch and is rubbing my nose in the fact that she had you first, I HATE it! Tell them that I am sick, I am going upstairs." With that she walked out and closed the door behind her. I stood there for a moment not knowing what to do, but thought of the note in my pocket. Pulling it out I read, "Justus, I doubt I will get a chance to talk privately with you, but I had to tell you some things. I wasn't prepared for how I would feel when I saw you had a girlfriend. When I left it was the hardest thing I ever had to do, but I wanted what was best for you, now I think it was the biggest mistake of my life. I know I still love you, and it kills me to think of you with another woman. There is so much I want to tell you, and something that you should know, but I am not going to write a novel. If you want to talk with me I am going to stay tomorrow night at the Holiday Inn. No one knows except you that I am staying there. I hope you will come by for a minute so I can talk to you, Janice."

I was stunned, what should I do? Should I go and talk to her? Did she know about what I had done to her husband? A million questions raced through my mind as I walked back to the kitchen.

"Debby isn't feeling good, so she went to bed."

"Well I hope she feels better in the morning, I guess I have had enough cards for one night anyway." Mom always thought about everyone else first and even though I knew she wanted to play cards she put them away.

"So Justus, tell me about some of your travels." Janice smiled a knowing smile as if she knew I had already read the note.

"Mom is probably sick of my stories by now."

"Of course I am not Justus, I love hearing about places you went. Sometimes I read your letters over and over just imagining what it would be like to travel somewhere different. I wanted to get upstairs and talk with Debby, but I also wanted to be here with Janice right now. I decided to stay and talk with Janice and mom for a while. Debby would get over it.

As the night passed it was fun to talk about the places I had been and the people I had met, and Janice seemed to really be interested. It was now getting late though and I wanted to talk to Debby.

"I am a bit tired, I think I am going to go to bed now."

"I am too son, I think it is a good idea for me as well."

"I might just have a snack before bed, if you don't mind Betty."

"Of course not Janice this is your house when you are here."

Mom headed into her room and I started to get up when Janice took hold of my arm.

"Did you read it?" I nodded, "will you come?"

I once again nodded that I would, she smiled and went to get a snack.

Quietly I walked up the stairs in case Debby was asleep.

"About time you decided to come up here." Her voice was cold and matter-of-fact.

"Did you really think I was just going to run up here? I think that would have been rude, besides I said you weren't feeling good, not me."

"If you cared you would have come up right away."

"Yes, if you were sick I would have been up here with you the whole time, but you aren't."

"Fine, I am not sick, just a bitch right?" I could tell she was getting mad now and I hadn't seen her ever mad.

"Debby, don't get upset, she will be gone tomorrow." All she said was that she wished she was gone now, then rolled over and didn't say another word to me that night.

The next day mom and Janice were up early, I could hear them talking from my room and Janice was telling my mom how she needed to get back home soon, but how much she enjoyed their visit. I decided to go down and say goodbye just before she left, I didn't want to go down and visit and only make Debby more upset. Just then she rolled over to face me, "aren't you gonna go down and visit with your girlfriend?" I hated sarcasm like this, and at first it made me kind of mad, then I tried to put myself into her shoes.

"You know she is not my girlfriend, don't act like that. I am sorry this had to happen, I don't want you to be upset."

"I will be fine when SHE is gone."

"I understand. I do have to at least go down and say goodbye though." She rolled back away from me.

"Whatever, I am not leaving this room until she is gone." I got dressed and went down when I heard Janice get ready to leave.

"Justus, I was thinking you weren't going to get up in time to say goodbye to me you sleepy head!"

"Of course I was, I am not that rude!" She winked and hugged me, I felt for a moment it was a previous time, when a hug was followed by 'I love you' and almost said it. Her perfume smelled so good at that moment and I had to pull away and put the impure thoughts out of my head. She looked at me winked and said, "hopefully we will get another chance to visit sometime soon." I said goodbye and went back to Debby.

"Good she is finally gone! It's about time."

"Why are you so threatened by her?" She got a look on her face that I knew I didn't want to hear the answer to, so I just told her never mind she is gone now.

The day was pretty routine and mom had to go have a treatment.

"Would you two mind coming with me today? I would really enjoy some company."

"I really need to change the oil on my car mom, can I come by a bit later?"

"Ok, but would you mind driving me Debby?" She agreed and soon they were out the door. I didn't really need to change the oil and although I hated to lie to them I had to find out what Janice needed to tell me.

I drove to the Holiday Inn and my stomach was in knots. Why was I so nervous? It wasn't like Janice and I were strangers, but I couldn't shake the feeling as I asked the desk clerk which room she was in. Knocking on her door I had the feeling I would be sick, but then she opened the door and seeing her standing there I suddenly felt better.

"I am so happy you came here Justus, I wasn't sure you would."

"I told you I would Janice, you should know I keep my word. Besides that I wanted to know what you had to tell me that was so important, what I should know about." She looked so nice and her smile was so bright until that second. She sat on the bed and her face became very serious, for a minute I thought she would cry and as she held back the tears I was about to find out something that I never could have imagined.

REGRETS

I went and sat next to her on the bed, "what's wrong? I'm sure it will be ok."

"No Justus it won't be, it can never be." Tears streamed down her face and she was having trouble getting the words out, "I'm sorry, give me a minute to compose myself." I put my arm around her and told her to take her time. I would wait until she was ok. At that she put her arms around me and told me how much she missed my compassion, how she always felt like she mattered when I was with her.

"But I couldn't ruin your life and had to let you go."

I still didn't understand how she would have ruined my life as she continued to speak.

"Justus I left because I was pregnant with your child." She suddenly blurted out. I didn't know what to say or do, it was unbelievable, I never in my wildest dreams imagined this.

"If I had stayed not only would everyone have found out about us, but I know you would have wanted to marry me and take care of your baby." Of course she was right, I would have never abandoned her.

"You are a loving caring man, that is why I never stopped loving you." It was obvious that she wasn't pregnant now, and I almost didn't want to ask this next question, but had to know.

"What happened?"

"As you know I was abused by my ex and lost my other child. I was told I could never get pregnant, remember?" Of course I did, but could only nod. She started to cry again and pulled close to me once more.

"I was 5 months along and lost your son, my insides were a mess and there was nothing they could do, he was just too small to make it. Now I know for sure I cannot have children, I lost the part of you I had hoped I would be able to love forever. Now I know I have also lost you forever as well."

I was all of a sudden aware that I was crying too, this was all so much to absorb and I couldn't speak.

"I hope you can forgive me, I never meant to hurt you." I could only pull her closer to me as the tears continued. She pulled her face back from mine and looked into my eyes as we both cried, a tiny smile appeared briefly on her lips. "You are the only man I have ever known that could cry in front of me." With her words she kissed me, and I found myself kissing her back.

All of my old feelings were awake for her again in an instant and I felt as if I were being washed down a raging river. My emotions were a tangled mess and all I wanted to do was feel better and make her feel better as well. Our kissing became more intense and the tears were replaces with sighs and her warm breath on my neck. Her skin felt so soft and smooth and the smell of her light perfume lingered still. Before I knew it we were undressed and I was inside of her, it felt so right and at that moment I completely forgot about all the stress I had been going through, mom and her cancer, and sadly even Debby. We made love and before I knew it 2 hours had passed.

"Oh my god, I told mom I was going to be at the hospital with her! I had better call or she will be worried." I dialed the hospital and when I had been transferred to her room was taken slightly back when Debby answered. Here I was in bed with Janice, and she was there with my mom. I felt just like one of the men whose life I had taken at that moment.

"Oh, hi Debby, can mom talk?"

"Yes of course, where are you?!?"

"I am so sorry, I was changing the oil when an old friend from school came by and I lost track of the time, I just now finished. As soon as I clean up I will be right there."

"No, don't bother, she is almost done then we will be home."

She sounded mad; I guess she had every right to be. How could I have done this to her? I tried to console myself with the fact that we weren't married, but I knew that was a lame excuse.

"Janice, I have to go, this should have never happened, I feel terrible."

"I know, but I don't regret it. I only wish I could be with you all the time. I miss you so much. I hope you can forgive me for all I have put you through."

"I know you only did what you thought was best, but were you ever going to tell me I had a son if you hadn't lost him?"

"Of course I was, but when he and you were older." As I dressed I wondered what difference it made, but perhaps in her eyes I was still a kid or something. "I wish I could stay and talk more, but I have to go."

"I know. You have a girlfriend." Her face once again saddened and she turned away from me. "Yes I do, I'm sorry Janice, I never wanted things to end like this for us, I never wanted us to end."

"It was my mistake, I have to live with it Justus, but know that I will always love you." I didn't want to say it, but it was the truth.

"Janice you were my first love, I will always love you too." Her eyes once again brimmed with tears, "you had better run, someone else loves you as well I am afraid." I turned and walked out as my mind raced with everything that had just happened.

I drove way too fast to get home and hoped I wouldn't get pulled over. Going into the driveway I could see they weren't home yet and ran to get into the shower. Although I wasn't dirty from changing the oil, I felt dirty all over and hoped I could keep behaving normally when Debby got back. I got out and began to dry off just as I heard the door.

"Justus honey we are back!" I heard mom announce.

"I am just getting out of the shower, be right out." I looked over to see the knob turning and pulled the towel around me.

"What..? You act like I have never seen you naked!" Debby grinned at me and pulled the towel away. I felt like she could see right through me, like there might be a sign painted on my skin that said I had been with another woman.

"Well you look pretty clean to me, I kinda wanted to see a bit of my dirty boy!" Winking she pulled herself against me. I felt like the dirtiest boy on earth at that moment but could only reply, "You seem to be in a better mood."

"Now that SHE is gone I am, you seem a bit distracted though, what's wrong?"

"Nothing really, my friend told me about a mutual acquaintance that had recently been killed in a car accident, it just made me think how life hangs by a thread."

"I understand, it is sad when good people die young, but some people should have died before they were born." I knew she was talking about her ex, but all I could think of at that moment was the son I almost had.

"Have you ever thought about having kids?"

"Where did that come from? Justus you are full of surprises aren't you!"

"So, have you?"

"Sure I guess so, but I am not ready at the moment, that is why I take birth control pills silly!"

"Obviously I don't mean right now, I was curious is all."

"That's cool, ask me again in a couple of years, ok?" She gave me a little smirk then walked out the door yelling back, get some clothes on you streaker! Your mom and I got fried chicken for dinner and it is getting cold."

She seemed back to her old self and my guilt was eating at me more than ever, what was I going to do? I knew I could never tell her, it would hurt her too much and accomplish nothing.

I remembered the day I shot my father, how I put it in my mind that it wasn't really me doing it, more like watching someone else do it. I would once again have to do the same thing now; I could never admit to myself that it had been me doing such a bad thing. I closed my eyes and visualized someone else in that hotel; I was here now, not there.

Mmm…fried chicken, I loved the fried chicken from our little local take out, and now that I had nothing on my mind to ruin my appetite I could enjoy my dinner.

Days passed uneventfully for a while, Debby and I were fine again and I did everything I could to keep Janice out of my thoughts. I still couldn't shake the feelings though and wondered if she was ok, wherever she was.

DESTINY

Mom was starting to feel better after a couple more weeks and Debby wanted to continue our travels before it started to get really cold.

"Justus, I have spent my life in the south, I would love to go west, see the Grand Canyon, maybe even the Pacific Ocean." I also wanted head west, and after talking to mom about our plans it was agreed that she would be fine without us there, and if there was an emergency I could always fly home.

Debby was excited to be back on the road and I knew I needed to put some of the events of the last few weeks behind me. As we drove seeing different places that make this country great like the Sears Tower, the St. Louis Arch, and the Alamo I thought about what men before me had done to make their mark in this world. I wondered what I would ever be able to leave as a legacy.

"Debby, do you ever wonder if when you are gone anyone will remember you?"

"I really have never thought of it, I don't have any close family and working as a waitress doesn't exactly make you famous, unless you are Flo! Maybe I should have told more people to kiss my grits!" It was funny the way she did the impersonation and I had to laugh at her being so silly. She tended to be more serious overall, but I understood that her life had not exactly been easy.

"I think it is too late to be Flo, but I am sure there is something we could do that we would be remembered for."

"What about you Justus? I bet there are things you are good at."

I thought about it for a minute, hmmm.. really the only thing of any consequence I had done was end the lives of some people that needed to die. Strangely enough this was something I felt pride in, I eliminated the source of suffering for a number of people and I would do it again.

"Debby I think the only thing I have done that amounts to anything was free you from your ex."

"That's true, and you kept me out of jail I'm sure. You really did give me life again."
She snuggled close to me as we drove across the desert southwest. I noticed a lot of
really run down houses with broken down junk cars and trash all over the yards, it
reminded me of Janice's house the first time I saw it.

"I wonder how many women and kids there are out there that are dealing with the
same thing you, my mom and so many others have had to put up with."

"I don't think I even want to know, it is so depressing." I had to agree with her, it was
a problem that would never go away and there was nothing I could do to stop it.

It was starting to get dark and I needed gas as we pulled off the highway.
There were plenty of run down gas stations that matched the rest of the town it
appeared. I started to fill up the tank as another car pulled in. This one looked like it
shouldn't even be running, rusty and with dents in almost every panel. I watched the
driver get out and speak to the woman passenger.

"Put a couple dollars in it, I am going to get some beer."

The woman getting out looked about as bad as the car, she was wearing a
dress that appeared to be 20 years old and was barefoot. A minute later the man came
out with his beer and walked up to the passenger side where she was putting the gas
in. "Dammit woman, you put five dollars in! I told you a couple, how goddamn
smart do you have to be to know that only means two?! Now I am gonna have to put
this beer back to pay for it!" With that he raised his hand and slapped her across the
face, for the first time I got a look at her face, but could only see my mothers face
instead. There was already a black eye, and a split lip, she didn't say a word, but
noticing me look at her only turned quickly and got back in the car.

"Hey what did you do that for?" I suddenly spoke to this piece of shit man that was
standing there.

"What's it of your business asshole?" The man started to walk towards me and I
stood my ground.

"You didn't need to hit her all she did was put in a little extra gas."

"Yeah well I didn't need to hit you either." His words were cut off as I found myself getting up off of the ground. At first things were hazy, but then came quickly into focus, I heard the car door slam and Debby yelling at him.

"What in the hell are you doing?" She came around the front of the car toward him; he turned to her and pushed her backwards. As she fell I thought about jumping up and tackling him, instead I went to her as he walked back inside.

"Are you ok Debby?"

"Yes I am fine, how about you?" Before I could answer the woman in the car spoke. "If I were you two I would get out of here, as you can see he has no problem hitting anyone, and I don't want to see you get it any worse. Please, just pull out back until he is gone, then pay for your gas."

I could see the look in her eyes; it was a look of terror. She was afraid for us, but for herself too. I was still a bit dazed and nodded to her, as I pulled the car around I could see him inside arguing with the clerk. I waited a few minutes and then watched as the junky car pulled back on the street.

"Come with me, let's see what happened." Debby and I walked in as the clerk stared at us.

"I thought maybe you two took off without paying for your gas for a minute, I was distracted by that asshole."

"No, we wouldn't do that, just decided to move the car before we paid."

"Looks like you did pay, you are going to have a nice shiner. I wish that guy would drive off a cliff or something; he is always trouble, comes in here drunk with pocket change and expects everyone to chip in so he can buy more beer. I have lost local customers because they don't want to run into him."

"Why don't you tell him to go somewhere else for his beer?"

"This is the only place in town close to where he lives, except the bar, and he is banned from going there."

"I can understand that, why don't you call the cops?"

"The only cop around here is a county sheriff that has too much country to cover and is sick of dealing with him, and no one ever presses charges, they are all afraid of him. Sadly the one that probably could do something is his wife, but as you might have noticed she is terrified of him, maybe more than anyone."

"Unfortunately I do understand. Why doesn't he get arrested for drunk driving? The sheriff could just hide and catch him when he comes in here at night drunk."

"Problem with that is he doesn't drive here, he walks. He only lives down the road."

"Well that sucks, I am glad I don't live around here. Lets hit the road Debby." We got back in the car and headed back to the highway.

"Debby, I know now what I am going to do, but when I tell you, you probably am going to think I am crazy and want to run for the hills."

"Justus, I would never do that, I love you and will be with you as long as you want me."

"Ok here goes, do you still have your gun?" Looking intently at me she nodded yes.

"I am going to kill that son of a bitch. Not because I am mad that he hit me, but when he pushed you it was all I could do to not run him over right there in front of that gas station. I am sick of hearing about men like him, there are too many, and I am not going to just sit on my hands anymore. " I waited for her to tell me that I was insane but instead she just replied, "How do you want to do it?"

I proceeded to tell her I figured it wouldn't be hard to find his house, we saw which direction he had driven off and the clerk said he lived close by. We would get off the highway at the next exit and circle back around to find his crappy car; then I would walk and wait between his house and the gas station.

"Justus, what if he recognizes you?"

"I want him to, and I want him to know why he is dying in the street like a dog."

"I understand, when I saw him hit you I felt like shooting him at that very moment."

We drove around to the next exit and after only a few minutes I saw the car. No surprises here, the house and the car were a perfect match.

"Justus, what if he doesn't go out? You know he couldn't get his beer today, he might be broke."

"You're right, I have and idea." I took a sheet of paper and wrote a note; 'I owe you something, and I always pay back'. Folding it around a five-dollar bill I quietly went up to the house and stuck it through a hole in the front screen door. "Ok Debby, take the car about half way to the gas station, I will be there soon." As she pulled away I threw a rock at the front of the house, hid and waited. A couple seconds passed then the door opened with a burst.

"Who the hell is out here!" It didn't take long for him to find the paper, I watched him open it and read the note and just as fast yell back in the house, "I'll be back in a minute."

I had hoped he would go back in to give me time to get closer to the car, but he was coming my way fast. I decided to make a run for it and hope in the dark he wouldn't see me. I had the gun in my hand and started to run. There was a van on the side of the road maybe a hundred yards from where I saw Debby park and decided to hide there. I was breathing heavy and nervous, but knew I needed to control this as thoughts of the day my father died came into my head. Before I could dwell on them he was close enough.

"Stop right there shit head!" I could see him freeze while he tried to see who I was.

"What's the matter, don't you recognize me?"

"Who the fuck are you?" He started moving forward as I cocked the pistol, hearing it he stopped again.

"You should have picked someone else's girlfriend to push on the ground."

"You're that kid from the gas station aren't you?"

"Yes, and this 'kid' has something to tell you, tonight was the last time you will ever raise your hand to another human being, a dog like you deserves to die like one and lay in the street."

"Why you smart ass little bastard, I am gonna kick the shit out of you."

Those were the last words he ever said; as he came toward me I fired straight into his chest. Stumbling backward he looked with surprise at the blood on his white shirt then fell on his back. The gun was surprisingly loud to me and I turned and ran as fast as my legs would carry me back to the car.

Debby later told me she couldn't see much, just that she saw a flash and heard the shot, then I was there.

She started the car and calmly drove back to the highway. We drove quietly for a while before she spoke.

"Do you think he is dead?" I hadn't even given a thought to the fact that he could still be alive and realized it wouldn't be hard for him to describe me, and the fact that I had spoken to the clerk would also give them an even better description.

"We have to find out, lets stay in this next town and see if there is anything on the news in the morning." Agreeing with me we pulled into a small motel and got a room.

"What was that like? I mean I thought about killing my ex many times, but never could, I was always too afraid until I met you." I had taken another life I was sure, and it didn't bother me at all, I would have felt worse killing a deer. To me the men I killed were ugly evil things, not even people. A deer was a beautiful graceful animal.

"I am not sure I can describe it, in a way I felt power, I had his life in my hands and with the movement of a single finger ended it. I don't feel bad at all for doing it either."

"I have never felt powerful in any way, well maybe lifting cases of food!" We both laughed at that and she hugged me, "I wish I could though."

"It is up to you, I hope you can handle it when the time comes."

"Someday I will surprise you, I know it is in me." Her words were said with feeling and I knew someday she would surprise me.

A NEW PLAN

I spent most of the night awake, wondering if he was dead, thinking about what I was going to do, and if Debby would really want to stay with me if he wasn't.

I drifted off and finally woke to the sound of the TV.

"Good morning sleepy head, it's almost 8. I felt you tossing and turning all night, did you sleep much?"

"A little, not great that's for sure. Maybe you can drive today."

"Sure, oh wait here is the news." The news anchor started with the story of a man who had been shot the next town over.

"This is it Justus," Debby said as they went to commercial. My question was soon answered.

"John Basset of Tucumcari was found shot to death on the street near his home, there doesn't seem to be a clear motive at this time and police continue to investigate." Debby turned off the tv and looked into my eyes, "I hope his widow can enjoy her life now, I know that no matter what happens she will be better off." I wondered if that was true, and decided to find out.

"Debby, does that phone book have listings for Tucumcari?" Looking at it she said it did.

"What was his name?" She asked. I had to laugh when I thought of it, "it was John Basset, like the dog!"

"Yes there is a John Basset listed here." I dialed the number and wondered if she would answer, before I thought of what I would say a woman's voice came on the line.

"Is this Mrs. Basset?"

"Yes it is, and if this is another reporter I have said enough already."

"No ma'am, I am someone that cares about you, and I just wanted to see if you are going to be ok now that your husband is dead."

"I am going to go stay with my parents for a while, but yes, I will be fine. Who are you?"

"A friend, someone who wants you to have a good life, a person that cares about people who have suffered like you. I would like to ask you a simple favor, the next time any news agency contacts you just tell them men like your husband will pay, justice is coming."

I hung up the phone and told Debby my plans.

"Remember when we were talking about leaving a mark on the world, being remembered for something? No one will know who I am, but I want my legacy to be spoken of as someone who cared about the abused and did something about it. You know as well as I do that the police can't, or won't do anything, these men are not going to change and will go from victim to victim, I am going to stop as many as I can from doing that."

"You're right Justus, it will never stop, but we are only two people how can we make any impact on a problem this big?"

"Like I just did, if she tells the news media what I said about justice coming, anytime I take matters into my hands I will leave a note that says simply, 'justice is coming'. If it stops abuse in one case, or gives one person hope, or the courage to leave, then it is better than not doing anything."

"There is only one problem with what you just said, WE are going to take matters into OUR hands. I know what it feels like to be on the receiving end of the abuse too, and I am with you until the end." I knew she meant it and agreed.

"How do we find the women and families that need us?" She asked.

" I have already thought of that, you will go to women's shelters as if you are currently being abused, talk with the other women and find out as much as you can, we will only be able to handle one or perhaps two in each town, then we will have to move on." She agreed it was a sound plan and would do it.

We decided to head to Albuquerque, a bigger city would be easier to blend into and we would be just another face. "This is going to be hard for you to do Debby, there are nights you will have to stay in different shelters, but you have to get to know at least some of the women. I will come to pick you up posing as your brother James and you can introduce me to whoever you think might be the right one."

Now I look back on this day as if it just happened, it is the day I found a purpose and the day that put me on my path to you, someone I never thought I would be telling all of this to, life is full of irony isn't it?

Anyway, that day we found a shelter and she checked in. I had no way to get in touch with her while she was there and told her to fake calling me the next day, but I would be there at noon.

"Debby, are you sure you can do this?" I asked her as she got out of the car. "You gave me life and I owe it to other women to have the chance I now have. Remember I love you and will be there for you always."

She was such a strong woman, and I thought back about when we first met and how I respected her then, it now paled in comparison.

My day was uneventful but I planned on how I would do things, I picked up supplies that would help me to reach success in each case, depending on the situation. Matches, lighter fluid, duct tape, a Swiss army knife, and assortment of other items. I got an inexpensive room for the night and watched TV. The eleven o'clock news came on and one of the stories was about the killing in Tucumcari.

"A strange story out of Tucumcari today, a man was gunned down in the street near his home, and while that is unusual, what has happened since then is even more bizarre. This was recorded earlier by our correspondent out of Santa Rosa."

"I am Kelly Jackson here in Tucumcari where we spoke with some of the neighbors about the killing that took place here last night. 'Sir, are you shocked by this in your town?'"

"By a killing yes, but the victim is no surprise at all."

"We got the same sort of response from many people here and it seems there is no remorse for this victim. The widow refused to be interviewed on camera but told us she had a strange call earlier in the day from a man that told her to only give this statement to the media, 'men like her husband will pay, justice is coming' reporting from Tucumcari this is Kelly Jackson."

I turned off the TV and was amazed that she had actually done what I asked. I drifted off to sleep and slept soundly having lost so much sleep the night before.

It felt odd to have breakfast the next morning without Debby there, this was the first time in as long as I could remember we hadn't started the day together and I missed her. I couldn't wait for noon to arrive, I wanted to be with her and was curious who she had met.

Finally I walked into the small building, "hello I am James, I am looking for my sister Debby."

"Yes she has spoken highly of you, come on back." It was not a big place but clean and brightly lit as if there was sunshine coming through many windows. I could see Debby in what I assumed was the main room talking with a very large dark skinned woman.

"James, I am glad you are here I will be ready to go in a minute, this is Carol maybe she can keep you company for a minute while I get my things."

"Hi Carol, nice to meet you." A weak smile came to her lips and she feebly shook my hand.

"Your sister speaks highly of you, she really loves you."

"She is a good sister, I just wish she could meet a good man."

"Don't we all, but they are few and far between."

I couldn't tell if Carol was black or possibly a mix of races, I only mention this to you because up until that moment I had met very few black people, there were none in my hometown and my dad was such a racist I had been brought up to fear them. Now here as I sat talking to this soft-spoken woman I didn't care what color she was. We made small talk for a few minutes and then Debby was back.

"It was nice to get to know you Carol, maybe someday we will meet again."

"That would be nice, but I hope it isn't in here."

Back in the car Debby told me about her. She was only 27, which surprised me I would have thought her much older, but as she continued I could see how her life had aged her beyond her years. She was married young, pregnant at 16, her boyfriend at the time mistreated her and she ran away from home. Ending up in New Mexico she had the baby but gave it up for adoption, her next boyfriend also got her pregnant, but he told her they should get married and keep the baby. He was much older and she thought it was a good idea, but the abuse started soon after the baby was born. She couldn't ever do anything right in his opinion, and a mistake meant being hit. She had 3 more kids by him and was sure it was only to keep her home and in his control. She began to eat compulsively hoping he wouldn't want to touch her sexually anymore, that worked, but the beatings got worse.

"Justus, this guy is a monster and she is going to die young if we don't do something to help her." I had already decided to help her when Debby told me her husband had said "she couldn't do anything right."

Those words still echoed in my head from when I was a child.

"I know where she lives, she wanted me to come by and visit."

"Good, lets see where it is."

This was obviously not the best part of town and I decided this would be a simple one

"I am just going to wait for him like before, let him know why he is going to die and end his miserable life. Let me out here, I need to see this asshole face to face." I walked up to the door and waited for him to answer. Instead a kid of about 7 opened the door.

"Who are you?"

"Hi my name is James, can I talk to your dad?"

"He isn't here, he is at Tyrone's."

" Where is that?"

"Just down the street on the corner." With that he shut the door. Getting back in the car I asked Debby what this guys name was. "Arthur, I gathered he is about 40, around 6ft tall and black." I had her leave me there and go get a room for that night then come back in about an hour.

The bar was dimly lit but I could see a guy at the counter that fit the description pretty well. I took a seat one over from him and ordered a beer. "You old enough for a beer kid?" The bartender chuckled as he poured me one. "I haven't seen you around here before, where you from?"

"Just passing through really, but I got in a fight with my girlfriend and she kicked me out of the car right outside!"

"What a bitch," the man next to me suddenly joined in, "dumb bitches, always trying to make our lives miserable!"

"There are times, that's for sure! My name is James." I held out my hand to him.

"I am Arthur." He said as he shook it. He had very strong hands and I could picture him hitting the poor woman I had spoken to a short time before.

"Kid you are too young to have to put up with a dumb broad like that, there are lots of women out there."

"I know, but I am stuck with her at the moment. What about you? You married?"

"Yeah, I got me a cow at home probably sitting on her fat ass doing nothing as usual."

" Well if you don't like her why not dump her?"

"Nah I need someone to take care of the brats, and do my laundry!" He laughed like a stupid hyena and I faked amusement.

"Besides, she does what she is told, I am the man in my house. You had better learn to act like a man or your woman will run your life!" Once again I flashed back to my father telling me to be a man like him. There was no doubt; this guy was a dead man.

A short while later Debby walked in, "There you are, I was worried about you."

Arthur looked at me and at her, "Remember what I told you kid."

"Oh trust me I won't forget what you said." We left and got back in the car

"Poor Carol, I can't imagine having to be with a creep like that. We need to wait for him to come out, lets just park over there by that alley, when he comes out I want you to lure him into it, tell him you met his wife and tell him what a piece of shit he is, I will come up behind him and that will be that.

We waited for a couple hours talking about Carol and how she would be without him. Debby told me how she got welfare and how that was probably another reason he kept wanting her to get pregnant, the more kids, the more money they got. He had been in the military and got some disability for some injury, but she knew he could work.

"Will she be alright financially with him gone?"

"She will still get the same money, but at least now he won't be there to drink it all away."

Just then I saw him come out, "quick get in the alley!" She ran back where the light was dim, but I could still see her. I ducked as he drew closer.

"Hey Arthur, come here."

"Who is that?"

"I am a friend of Carols, come here." His back was now to me as he walked in the alley.

"So what the hell are you doing in an alley? You want to give me a blow job or something?!" His words were slurred and he grunted out a laugh.

"NO asshole, I want you to know that she wished you would die, and tonight her wish comes true."

"What? Who is going to do that to me... you? Stupid little girl, I think you need to learn some respect!" The tone of his voice was menacing and he moved closer to her as I called his name.

"Hey Arthur!" He turned back to me.

"Where in the hell did you come from?"

"No, I didn't come from hell, but it is where you are going, you should have listened to her, today your wife's wish comes true."

He charged at me as I fired the gun, the first shot only slowed him and I quickly pulled the trigger twice more, he fell at my feet and for a moment I had the thought he was going to get me before I got him.

"Get in the car Debby quick!" She ran to the car as I pulled a piece of duct tape off the roll where I had written 'Justice is coming', taped it to his back and ran to the car as Debby slammed down the accelerator.

WAS IT WORTH IT?

As I already mentioned my father was a racist among his other wonderful qualities. He used the 'N' word regularly and I found it offensive therefore virtually never used it.

I don't imagine it is in your vocabulary either, but this is one time I did use it, since he was such a disgusting person.

"Holy crap Debby, that big nigger almost got me! We need a bigger gun." I exclaimed as we sped away.

"I know, I was really scared for a minute too."

"Maybe we should get a shotgun and saw the barrel off." She agreed with me and drove us back to where she had gotten a room that night.

We heard on the news the next morning about how they had found the body and the message on duct tape attached to it. It would only be a matter of time before everyone knew about us.

Over the next couple of years this scenario repeated itself, she would find someone that was in an abusive, possibly life threatening situation and I would set it up in one way or another so their abuser got the justice he deserved. If they would benefit from the house burning down I would do that, leaving a note in a mailbox, or somewhere that it wouldn't be destroyed.

We had been on the west coast for a while and there were no shortages of opportunities to rectify things for those we could. I began to notice some things as time went on. As our deeds became more widely known and I was dubbed 'The Justice Killer' cases of abuse started to fall. There were even a few instances of killings that were blamed on me, but I was nowhere near the area.

Debby and I always assumed maybe some family member had had enough, and decided to end it themselves. Regardless of who did it, there was no end of talk anytime Debby was in a women's shelter. Many of the women that ran them said ladies they had seen regularly finally got the courage to leave their abuser. The women would say they weren't afraid anymore. We also began to recognize a lot of these poor women had gone from one bad relationship to the next. Many of them would tell Debby about the need to feel wanted, no matter what the consequence. Now they were beginning to feel they could be strong and independent, there was someone out there that cared about them.

One day I decided to call mom and see how she was doing.

"Hi mom, how are things there?"

"I wish I could say wonderful, but I have been feeling sick again. Janice volunteered to come stay with me and help out and I am so thankful for it."

"Do you want me to come home for a while until you feel better?"

"No dear, I will be fine, I am used to this by now. I think having her here is more for the company than anything else. Hang on a minute she wants to say hello."

I didn't know what to say, the last time we had talked was over two years ago, the day I cheated on Debby, I really wanted to forget about it.

"Hello Justus, how have you been?" She caught me off guard with how quickly she was on the line and I stammered "good, enjoying the California weather."

"You still have the same girlfriend?"

"Yes she is here with me, how about you? Anyone special in your life?"

Part of me wanted her to say yes, but deep down I wanted to hear a 'no'.

"No Justus, I can't seem to find a man that measures up to the man I still love, and I suppose I am always going to be afraid to get into another relationship."

"I'm not exactly sure what to say to that, but you are a strong woman and can't live your life being afraid now, the past is over."

"That has always been a two edged sword for me, part of my past I want to forget, and another part I never want to. Anyway it was nice to talk with you, here is your mom again." Mom went on to tell me about her treatments, how she was so sick of them, and how she missed me. I missed her as well and wanted to go visit soon.

"Debby, what do you think about giving this all up and going back home?"

" Actually Justus I have been thinking about that a lot lately, sometimes all of this is so depressing. I know we are helping a lot of women and kids to have a better life, but I want a life that isn't always moving around. I feel part of me is dead, I have had to suppress my emotions so much."

I had to agree with her, she was much more distant lately and the rare nights we were together we rarely made love. I felt like she was a stranger a lot of the time. Worse was that I felt I drank more than I used to and hated the feeling I was using it to blind me to the ugliness around me.

"I think this is catching up with me too and it is only a matter of time before we get caught, lets get out of here."

We took off right then and headed east. I wanted to try and find the relationship we once had, so I stopped at different places along the way that I thought were beautiful. It didn't seem to matter to her; she was not the same and didn't care. I felt like I had put her through too much, month after month of hearing horror stories that must have just reminded her of all she had been through before she met me.

"Debby, you know that Janice has been staying with my mom don't you?"

"No, not until now, why didn't you tell me?"

"I guess I hadn't thought about it really, but now that we are getting close to home I was reminded of it."

"You can call your mom and have her tell her to go back to where she came from, we are going to be there, she doesn't need HER around anymore."

"Oh Debby, don't get like that, you have nothing to worry about."

"I realize that Justus, but try to put yourself in my shoes, think how you would feel...remember?"

I did remember and really didn't want them to even see each other, so I agreed to call mom first chance I got. I spoke with her at the next gas station and told her how it wouldn't be necessary for Janice to stick around anymore, Debby and I would be happy to take care of whatever needed to be done. She was hesitant but agreed that

Janice probably wanted to go back to her home anyway. As we pulled in the driveway it always seemed like such a surprise

That everything looked the same, it was comforting though and I was glad to be back home. Mom came out and greeted us with a hug.

"I have really missed you Justus, and it is of course a pleasure to have you back again also Debby."

Heading inside the smell of home cooking filled my nostrils, I had forgotten how much I enjoyed being here. Debby wanted to shower and clean up so mom and I sat at the kitchen table and talked.

"Son, you look so much different, I am not sure exactly what it is, but you seem much older."

I could only imagine what changes she could see. I felt in the last two years I had aged ten.

"I hope I don't look terrible or something!" I had to joke with her and lighten my mood.

"No dear, just more mature I guess. Before I forget I have something for you." She got up and got an envelope off the desk. "Janice left this for you."

"I wonder why she would do that?"

"Justus, you know I have always respected you, and you have been mature beyond your years for as long as I can remember. I have never pried into your private life, but I am also not a naïve fool."

"Of course you aren't mom, I would never think something like that." I wasn't sure what she was leading up to but the mystery was soon solved.

"Justus, I know about you and Janice, I have known for a long time."

My mouth dropped and I started to dispute her, but she continued. "Please don't deny it, I am not mad and I don't condemn either of you, it should be obvious that I still care a great deal for her. While morally I don't condone things like sex before marriage, I will not put my religious views in your face. I think you believe in God, so that is enough for me now."

I didn't know what to say, but thanked her for being a good mother and not judging either of us.

The bathroom door opened and I quickly shoved the letter in my pocket.

"I think you could use a shower too Justus, you smell bad!"

"Oh thanks for pointing that out with such tact!" I gave a little laugh, but she just looked at me as if to say 'are you going to take one or not?' I went into the bathroom and pulled out the note remembering the last time I was in there reading a note and how Debby came in, and how playful she was, I was really starting to miss that girl. We had both became harder and colder, and I didn't like it. I began to read.

"Dear Justus, I had hoped to see you when you got back but your mother told me how your girlfriend wouldn't like it. You know how much I miss you and care about you, this is very hard for me to just leave, but I want you to be happy. I think everyday how things could have been different for us, how I could have had the chance to be happy too, but we all make decisions that affect our lives, either reaping the reward, or paying the consequences. I hope all of your decisions give you rewards, but no matter what I will be here for you if they don't, and will support you to the end. My phone number is at the bottom and also my address if you ever get up this way. You know you still have all my love, Janice."

In a way it surprised me that she still loved me so much, but I also knew that deep down inside I would always love her too. I folded the note up and put it in my wallet.

Mom's treatments were again going well and true to my promise I continued to shave my head until the day she got better. It was funny to me now to even see pictures of me with hair, mom of course wore wigs and I think she enjoyed the variety they offered her. She seemed happy, and even though there were days that she felt obviously worse, she never once complained. Debby on the other hand seemed to be increasingly frustrated and sullen.

"Debby, what's wrong? I thought that when we got back here you would be happy, but you only seem sad all the time."

"Justus, I don't know what is wrong, I feel like sometime we made the wrong choice, almost all of my money is gone now and I don't know what to do with my life. I know you are happy to be here but what are you going to do? I don't think either of us wants to go back to restaurant work, and I have no skills. I am confused and depressed."

I hadn't given any consideration to the future it seemed; now it was here in front of me and I had no idea what I was going to do either. She was right, what would we do now?

The days moved slowly by and Debby seemed to grow more distant, I wanted to fix it, but didn't know where to begin. I went back to the store where I used to work and they gave me a job. I only wanted it to be temporary but at least there would be some money coming in. Debby helped my mom around the house and went with her to the hospital when I couldn't for her treatments. I felt bored and wanted to feel the rush and excitement again that I had felt so many times the last couple years. I wondered if maybe I was crazy to think of killing as a rush of excitement, but the fact was I did feel that. Now I was home and wasn't going to start doing that again, if mom were ever to find out it would destroy her.

What could I do to feel alive again? Then it hit me.

"Hi Janice, how are you?"

"Justus! I am so happy you decided to call me, I really didn't think you would."

"I couldn't get you out of my mind, I had to see how you were doing."

"My life is pretty dull really, so not a lot."

"Sounds like me lately, I am not used to doing nothing. I like being home, but I need some excitement I guess."

"I couldn't agree more, why don't we meet for lunch or something and you can at least tell me about all the exciting things you have done these last couple years?"

I thought about it for a minute, I knew Debby would be upset, but then again lately I didn't even think she cared about me at all.

"Sure Janice, I would love to catch up with you." Maybe not surprisingly she had already thought of a restaurant about half way between our houses. I agreed I would meet her the next day.

On the way home I thought about what I would tell Debby, I usually had Sunday off.

"Hi, I am home. Where is everyone?"

"Hello dear, we are upstairs, Debby was showing me some pictures."

I went upstairs and joined them as mom continued.

"You two didn't take many pictures this last year, you must have been busy!"

I hadn't thought about it, but we both kind of had lost our zeal for seeing the sights, and looking at the beauty around us. We had spent so much time trying to correct the ugliness it had attached itself to us now.

"I guess we just got used to the area and forgot to take pictures." I suggested. They finished with the album they were on and mom volunteered to start dinner. As she walked downstairs Debby spoke to me, "it is strange how we started with taking pictures of everything, and at the end we didn't even take one picture on the trip home. Why is that? What happened, when did it all change?"

I didn't know what to say, but she was right, we were strangers now.

"I don't know what happened, but we can work it out." She told me she still loved me and wasn't going to give up that easily. I remember thinking at the time that she just didn't have anyplace better to go.

"I have to work tomorrow Debby, one of the guys is sick." As I spoke I thought about how it used to bother me to lie to her, but now I felt nothing. I had become hardened.

I imagine you think I have ice running through my veins, maybe you are right, but for a brief time I once again felt alive.

I got up the next morning, told Debby goodbye and headed out to meet Janice. I felt excitement and anticipation that put a smile on my face for the first time in a long while. Usually when I felt like this I was deadly serious, and of course someone would end up dead. As I neared our rendezvous point I felt my hands sweaty on the wheel.. wow, it was like being a teenager again! I pulled in just as Janice did; she saw me and gave me a big smile as we parked side by side. Getting out she ran over to me and gave me a huge hug.

"I have missed you so much! God you look wonderful, you even have a tan on that sexy bald head." She continued to smile as she rubbed it for a second.

"Hey, you are going to make me blush!" It had been a long time since I had done that, but at that moment I remembered how it felt.

"You hungry cutie?" She didn't wait for an answer but took my hand and walked me toward the restaurant. We got a booth in the corner and talked about everything that had happened the last couple years, after an hour or so she looked me straight in the eye and asked me, "Justus, do you regret making love to me that day at the Holiday Inn?"

"Wow Janice, that was out of the blue, what brought that up?"

"We are not children Justus, and I want to know if you regretted it, and if not I wondered if you would like to be with me again... today."

She was right, we were not children, and although I regretted it for a while, I didn't now.

"No Janice, I don't regret it. But I am with Debby still, doesn't that bother you?"

"I don't care about her at all, and I have an idea your feelings aren't that strong for her anymore. If they were, I don't think you would be here now." I had to agree with her, I hated the way things were between Debby and myself lately, and I wished things could have been different, but we made our choices.

"You are too smart for your own good Janice, you're right. I don't know what happened, we have been in the same bed, but miles apart for a while now, I hate it."

"Then come with me now, you can feel what it is like to be with someone that has love and passion for you." I didn't say anything back to her, left some money on the table, and took her hand this time and led her out the door.

There was a motel next to the restaurant and a few minutes later we were kissing passionately the way we used to. I remembered her soft skin and the same subtle hint of perfume on her as I took her clothes off. She trembled at my touch and slight gasps that were barely audible came through her lips as

my hands lightly touched her body. She began to simultaneously remove my clothing and as she did all of my senses came back to life. I felt like the whole world was going in slow motion, every touch, breath, and movement seemed to last forever.

Easing her onto the bed she slowly put me inside of her and all the control I thought I had exploded in an instant. Pulling me closer to her she didn't say a word, just held me as I felt our hearts racing.

"Janice," I finally spoke, "I can't remember when I have felt so complete. I can't explain it, but I don't want it to end."

"That is up to you, I am yours if you want me." I knew I did, but what about Debby? Maybe she wouldn't even care, she didn't seem to want me anymore. We hadn't even made love in weeks. I didn't know what to do at that moment and just kissed Janice one more time.

"I have to go, I don't want to, but until I can figure this out I don't want anyone to know about us."

"I trust you Justus, I will wait for you." I knew she was telling the truth, and she proved it beyond any question. I drove home thinking about all that this day had brought. I never stopped loving her; it was foolish to deny it anymore. I hadn't lied to Debby, I really loved her as well and for a time she helped me to forget the pain in my heart, but now I had to find a way to end our time together. I told myself that she would be fine with it; I mean if she really wanted me then why hasn't she wanted me in bed? It was obvious to me she just needed a reason to move on with her life.

I pulled into the driveway and noticed I was a bit late.

"It's about time Justus, we thought you were not going to get here for dinner." The thought occurred to me that if they had called the store everything would hit the fan, but apparently neither one had.

"Sorry, had a bunch of things to do that took me longer than I thought they would."

"It happens," was all Debby said. We ate and the usual small talk was there, I was thinking of the day and the feelings that were renewed in my body and mind. I should have felt guilty perhaps, but didn't, I felt alive for a change and was not going to give it up.

"Justus, do you have to work tomorrow?"

"Yes mom, Monday is the delivery truck, so it will be a long day."

"Debby had plans and wasn't going to be able to drive me to the hospital tomorrow, I just wondered if you had the chance."

"I wish I could, but I have to be there for sure, where are you going Debby?"

"I just needed to head to Fort Wayne to get some things, I haven't been shopping in forever and my clothes are so worn out."

"Can't you do it after I get off work?"

"Do you really want to sit there while I try on bras...? No, I didn't think so."

"Ok, leave the sarcasm outside, I got it." I was a bit upset that she couldn't even drop mom off and then go, but I wasn't going to argue with her.

"Hey you two, I am a big girl, I can drive myself. I just like the company is all."

"I know mom, sorry we didn't mean to make you feel bad."

Debby and I didn't talk much that night, she just watched tv for a while and then went to bed, by the time I came up she was already asleep. I remembered the times when she would go out of her way to see me; how she would do anything just to be with me. Now... nothing. I decided tomorrow night I would tell her things were not going to work out for us. I got up early the next morning as usual while she slept. I thought of when she and I ate breakfast together, now it seemed like a million years ago. After I ate I went up and woke her, "Debby, you will have to take me to work if you want the car."

"Oh, yeah, ok" she mumbled as she rolled over.

"Hurry up, I don't want to be late."

"Fine, you won't be late, I am up!" I walked downstairs shaking my head, it was over for sure, I didn't have a doubt.

Dropping me off she just drove away, I again thought of the days when she would never leave without saying "I love you" and then I thought of Janice and how she never stopped loving me.

I was working like a maniac trying to keep up with the guys unloading the truck when I looked up to see the sheriff. 'Oh Crap!' I thought, what was he doing here? My criminal life flashed in front of me as he spoke.

"Hello Justus, it's been a while." His face was deadly serious and I wondered what he would say next.

"I need to talk to you, privately." We made our way to the break room as he began to speak.

"Justus...." his eyes were suddenly full of tears "there has been an accident...your mother... your mother... was involved."

My heart stopped, "where is she! Is she ok?!"

"Justus... she's gone. A semi ran the light, he apparently had fallen asleep, your mother died at the scene."

"NO, NO!!! You are wrong! You have to be wrong!!!" I fell to my knees and put my head on the bench, this couldn't be happening, there had to be a mistake.... there of course was no mistake, and I lost my mother that day.

GOD'S FAULT?

I couldn't stop crying, I was aware of people coming in, the sheriff asking them to leave, but I didn't care. I wanted to wake up, this had to be another nightmare. It wasn't though, and as I slowly raised my head sometime later there was only a puddle of tears and reality.

I figured in some way this was God's doing, maybe to teach me a lesson or something, and I hated him for it. I am sure to you that is a foolish notion, but it is how I felt at this moment.

The sheriff was still there and he walked over to me putting his hand on my shoulder.

"Justus, I have been around here for a long time and have seen you grow up, you have been through some hard times I know, but you are strong and will get through this too." Sheriff Clark was one of the few men in this world that I respected and believed to be a good human being.

"Thank you Tim, I guess in some ways you are like family to me. Is there any way I can see her?"

"Justus, right now you don't want to, but she will be ready at the funeral if you want it that way." I had to see her one more time, I had to say goodbye and told him so.

"Do you need a ride home Justus?" I had forgotten until now that Debby had my car so I agreed and followed him out to the patrol car.

We drove in silence to my house with only the police radio breaking in once in a while. My thoughts and emotions were a jumble of sorrow, anger and hatred. I just wanted to keep crying but the thought of the accident made me angry that someone was too tired to drive but still continued. I was angry at Debby too, if she had driven mom to the hospital this wouldn't have happened either. Finally I thought about how I had taken her husbands life, drugged him with sleeping pills and killed him in his semi. This had to be God getting even with me I thought at that moment.

We pulled into the driveway and I thought how it would never be the same again, how could I ever be happy in this house without her here? I started to cry again and Tim waited patiently for me to get out.

"I'm sorry sheriff, I am sure you have important things to do."

"Don't worry about that Justus, and you can still call me Tim if you like." I got out of the car and thanked him as I slowly walked toward the door.

Through my tears everything was a blur and I thought about how the last few years of my life seemed like this too, everything at that moment was an unfocused mess to me. I lay down on the couch not wanting to ever get up, at some point I must have fallen asleep because the sound of the door closing woke me.

"Justus, what are you doing here? I thought you were going to be working late." I looked up at her and again felt how none of this would have happened if she had driven. Any feeling I had for her was now completely gone and I didn't even want her there right now.

"Are you ok? What's wrong?"

I just blurted out to her, "Mom's dead, she was killed in a car accident." She dropped her bags to the floor and stood motionless for a minute, then started toward me. I didn't want her to come any closer and said bluntly, "if you had driven her she would still be alive!"

Stopping in her tracks she stared at me for a moment, "how can you blame me? If I had driven we might both be dead."

In hindsight this was a possibility I have to admit, but I didn't want to think about that at this time and told her I wanted to be alone. She picked up her bags and went upstairs, while I sat there a hollow shell of the man I thought I was. I once again was that scared little boy, needing his mommy, but this time she wouldn't be there; she would never again be there for me. I didn't get to be a little boy again, any part of me that was died that day too.

The next couple of days were a blur of responsibilities and things I didn't want to deal with. From funeral arrangements to insurance agents I had to keep being reminded of her being gone. The day after the accident I called Janice and told her what had happened, I think possibly she cried as much as I did and I wished I could have been there for her. I don't know if Debby cried at all, and it just reaffirmed to me that she had no feeling anymore. The funeral would be in a few days. I told Janice I wanted her to be there, she of course agreed. The truck driver that killed mom wasn't even slightly injured and Tim told me that he wanted to speak with me, to apologize. I wanted to tell him that I wished he was dead too, but instead refused to see him. His insurance paid for the funeral and I would receive an insurance check for the accident, but I could care less.

The weather was typical for this time of year, it was cold and overcast, the snow hadn't started yet but the day of the funeral it felt as if the whole world was gray and frozen. Janice had come in the night before and I told Debby point blank that she would be at the funeral, and sitting next to me.

"She was my mom's only friend for a long time and she is family, I will not put up with any kind of jealous displays."

"I won't, trust me." She had become more distant the last few days and I could tell she didn't even want to be in the house with me. I slept on the couch and we hardly spoke.

As we entered the funeral home I was surprised at the amount of flowers that were there. I walked in to where the body was and was unprepared to see Janice already there. Her back was toward us but I knew it was her, as did Debby. I continued in, Debby stopped there. As I drew closer I could see Mom's face, and the tears ran uncontrollably down my cheeks. I walked up next to Janice, she turned slightly toward me and I could see the front of her dress was soaked as she continued to cry.

"Oh Justus, I am so sorry" she said as she put her arms around me and her body convulsed as she wept on my shoulder. After a minute I pulled back and asked her to give me a few minutes alone, she agreed and walked to the back of the room.

"Mom, I don't know where to start, I wish I had been here more the last couple of years, I would give anything to erase what I have done, to be the son you needed. I gave you a new life and then left you alone, I know you were being selfless in letting me go, but now I can never get the time back. Please forgive me and know that I have always loved you more than anyone, you gave me life and you protected it for years, thank you for loving me and being my mother."

I turned and tried to compose myself, I knew there would be people coming and I had to meet them at the door. Janice and Debby were both toward the back of the room still, although on separate sides. The funeral director told me I would be up front and then escorted them to where they would be sitting, with only my chair between them. I didn't have time, or care to see what, if anything they had to say to each other as the guests started to arrive. I was once again surprised at the number of people who came in, Mom had made a lot of friends the last few years along with the people she had met and grown to know at the hospital. The few relatives we had made the trip, Linda and her husband along with a few others I barely knew.

I took my seat between the ladies as the preacher started to speak. He mostly went on how things happen for a reason and how God needed my Mom for something special, I realize this was supposed to make me feel better, but instead I was just mad again because I needed my Mom there with me. He had asked me before if I wanted to say anything and I told him yes, he now called me up to speak. I walked up and looked out on mostly faces of strangers, but I knew they all must have loved my Mother or they wouldn't be there. I choked back my tears and talked about how she had made nothing but sacrifices her whole life, how she was a kind, giving, loving woman and each one of them must have known that. How she smiled in the face of adversity and fought against the cancer for years. "I loved my Mom every day of her life and would have done anything she asked, she never did ask much as a lot of you know, so I will ask for her. Please take care of each other, live each day as if it were your last, love those who love you and try to never do anything that would hurt them."

The rest of the day is like a fog to me, we went to the grave sight and I watched them lower her down into the earth. Debby said very little and only that she was sorry, Janice drove behind us and told me as we left the cemetery that she would be in town for a couple of days if I needed to talk. Debby and I went back to the house and I fell asleep on the couch as I had for the last few nights. Morning came with me waking to see Debby standing above me, a couple of suitcases next to her on the floor.

"Justus, I need to go, nothing will ever be the same for us. I know you blame me for your mother's death, and even without that we have grown apart. I do still love you but you are not happy with me, so what's the point? Maybe someday you will feel differently, but now I know you don't love me."

I was somewhat surprised, but at the same time thought it was the right thing to do.

"Where are you going to go?"

"For now back home to that crappy little town where you met me, I am sure I can get my old job back until I figure out what to do. A cab is going to take me to the bus depot, so you don't have to get up, don't worry about me, I will be fine." She bent down and kissed my cheek and walked out. I lay there alone as the morning light came through the window, I never felt so alone.

HAPPINESS

I don't know if you have ever lost someone you were close to, but unless you have it is not something I can describe. I suppose you could imagine yourself losing one of your senses, you know what it was like to have it, now it is gone.

Debby leaving was not a big surprise to me, but again she was someone I was used to being around, and now she was gone as well. I didn't want to get up, I could have just laid there and died I thought more than once, but being a human being my stomach eventually made me get up and eat something. Looking around the kitchen I started to notice all the little things Mom had done since dad died. There were cute curtains in the window, she had put a wallpaper border with flowers on it near the ceiling, and there were some little animal knickknacks on top of the cabinets. I thought it was odd how I had never looked at any of this before.

We take everything for granted, assuming nothing will ever change, it may be one of the greatest weaknesses we have as people.

As I pondered this I decided I wouldn't be guilty of it again. I got dressed and drove to talk to Janice.

"Hi Janice, are you busy?"

"I am never too busy to talk to you, you know that." I did, she was the one person on earth that I really believed would drop everything just to talk to me.

"Janice, I have been thinking a lot today, actually for a while now...hmm... how can I put this?" She interrupted me.

"Justus, just tell me what is on your mind, I know the last few days have been hard for you and I want you to feel like you can tell me anything."

"Ok, I guess what I really want to say is... would you like to come and stay at the house with me?" She looked a bit shocked, but there was the hint of a smile on her face.

"What about Debby?"

"She is gone, to tell you the truth she has been gone for a while, at least emotionally."

"I would love to stay with you, you already know that though."

She was right, I did know, but I didn't want her to feel like I wanted her there just to keep me from being alone and told her so.

"Justus, I would move heaven and earth for you and even if that was all you wanted or needed I would be there." I thought about how wonderful it would be to have her with me again, and how I knew I could make her happy, I felt as if my life once again had a meaning, and a purpose.

"Would you like to come up north with me to help me get my things? I don't really have a lot, I rent a furnished apartment so mostly it would be clothes and some personal stuff." I was happy to go with her and told her 'lets go right now', which she gladly agreed to.

We dropped her car off at my house and took mine since it was bigger. The drive only took a couple of hours, but talking with her and having her sit next to me made the time fly by. It was the first time in days I didn't think about Mom being gone and feel like I would start crying again.

She had a nice apartment spotlessly clean and very homey. There were a number of hand knitted blankets on the couch and I couldn't help but notice how beautiful they were.

"Where did you get these?"

"You are going to think I am an old lady or something, but I made them. I don't do much in this town, but like to knit while I watch TV sometimes."

"I of course don't think you are an old lady, and admire your skill and the beauty of what you have made." She smiled broadly and gave me a huge hug, "Oh Justus, you always know exactly what to say; you are so sweet!" I put my arms around her and felt the stirring of my senses once again, "Janice you make me feel alive, I missed you more than you know." Without a word she only pulled her face back from mine and looked into my eyes as I saw more than words could ever express.

"Ok, we had better get this started, or we will never get done!" She turned and began to put things into the boxes we had gotten. I stopped myself for a minute and took a look around; I wanted to start to take in my surroundings, to be more observant. Although her place was immaculate, I didn't see much in the way of personal items, other than the afghans at first. Then I did start to see, there were pictures here and there, of her and I on my birthday the night we first were together, in fact counted 11 pictures either on the walls, or on her dresser. Each one was of her and my Mom, her and I, or all three of us. There was not one other. I began to realize that we were her only family and how my loss was also hers, and never doubted for a minute after that how she and I would be together until the end.

We stayed there that night and in each other's arms found a joy I had doubted was ever going to be possible again. The next day I awoke with a sense that my life was just beginning, we finished packing and headed back to 'our' house. Janice never tried to change anything at the house; she wanted to remember my Mom as much as I did. She would add touches here and there so it felt like our home, but that was all. We both loved to take walks back in the woods and she would take pictures of me, and I of her in the snow.

I occasionally thought of the last time I had been in these woods, and how it was a million miles away from how I felt now. I was home and with the woman I loved.

If there was a way to describe pure contentment, happiness, joy, and zeal for life, I would do it now, but all words pale in significance to what I felt.

I kept my job at the store and they soon made me assistant manager, Janice took the job my Mom had been doing and since she had been there before had a lot of old friends to catch up with. The tedious things of life such as doing dishes or cooking a meal became events to me, I had her next to me and we did everything together. I would look forward to getting off work, going to the fabric store and waiting for her as she would help the last customer of the day. I sometimes wondered why she even worked there, I made a good wage, and the money from the insurance I received after the accident was plenty, but she enjoyed it and I wanted her to do what made her happy.

The winter melted away and spring came early, she and I went and bought a bunch of flowers that she could plant and at the same time decided to start a little garden to grow vegetables. I helped her plant the flowers and the seeds for the garden.

I am sure to you this all sounds incredibly boring, but for me it was one of the few times in my life that I felt truly and completely happy. I was in love and so was she, and although I had loved Debby, Janice was my first love and I knew would be my last.

The summer gave way to fall and Janice and I had a friend take pictures of us with the beautiful colors all around us, I remember telling her how all the beauty of nature paled next to her, I know it sounds corny, but it was the truth from my heart.

We were outside one day getting the rest of the vegetables from the garden when a strange car pulled in.

"Who is that Justus?" I had no idea and told her as we both walked to the driveway. The driver got out and we both stopped in our tracks.

"Debby? What are you doing here?" Janice took my hand and held it tight.

"I was in the area and thought I would stop by to see if you missed me, but I can see you don't." I didn't know what to say and just stood there like a fool while Janice spoke.

"It was nice of you to stop by and see if Justus was ok, but as you can see he is fine, we are both very happy and really don't want company tonight." She was very matter of fact, and in this case I appreciated it. Debby didn't even look at her, but spoke to me.

"Is that true Justus, you are perfectly happy here now and don't want any company?" I didn't like her putting me on the spot and let her know.

"Yes Debby that is true, I am happy and would rather not have company at this time."

"Wow, it must be wonderful to be 'perfectly happy' I don't know what that is anymore. I seem to have a hard time being that happy, lots of things bother my conscience. Hey Justus, did you ever tell her about all of our travels? Did you tell her about all the people we met along the way? I am sure she would love a nice bedtime story."

"Debby, that is ancient history and you know it, please just let it go."

She got back in her car and drove away, but Pandora's Box had been opened, and there was no way to close it now. Janice looked at me as she drove off, "what did she mean, what is she talking about?" I could see my wonderful life evaporate in front of my eyes.

"Do you trust me?"

"Yes, with my life."

"I will tell you everything, but I am afraid you won't love me anymore. It isn't good." She looked me in the eye as she had done so many times before.

"I will love you until the day I die, no matter what."

The next few hours she learned what only Debby and I knew, I kept waiting for her to freak out, to run away or something, but she just listened.

"Did you kill my ex husband?" I hadn't expected this question, but could only take her hands in mine, "yes Janice, I did." Her eyes never left mine.

"Justus, I am not sure what to say, I have always hated violence, but you gave me the chance to be happy, I think you gave a lot of people the chance to be happy, I love you and will never bring this up again if that is what you want." I could only nod and put my arms around her.

"I hope you understand why I hadn't told you about any of this. I wanted to put it in my past and never think about any of it again. I thank you for understanding and It will never come up again."

I would have given anything in the world for that statement to have been true, but it was out of my hands, if only I had known. A couple days later a car pulled into the driveway, this time I did recognize it and went outside.

"Debby, why are you here?"

"Because I wanted to know if SHE left yet?" I hated the way she always referred to Janice as 'SHE' or 'HER' with a grimace on her face and told her so.

"Oh, I see you are defending the woman that took my place, is she better than me? Are you happier with her?" It was like being on trial.

"I am not going to compare the two of you, I am happy as I said before, and she is still here with me."

"Enjoy it then Justus, life is never fair." Janice came out as she finished speaking, "I hope you have enjoyed being with a killer, see you later." Janice started to speak, but Debby got into her car and drove away.

"What the hell is wrong with her? What did I do to make her hate me?"

"You didn't do anything wrong, you just loved me and that is too much for her. "Justus, I'm afraid, what if she keeps coming around here, you told me she had a gun."

"Don't worry, she knows I will defend you, and I don't think she will hurt me." I was wrong.

AT WHAT PRICE?

I had no idea of what Debby was thinking, I couldn't understand why all of a sudden she was so concerned with me, it was not that long ago that she left and didn't seem to care. Now Janice was afraid and I had to wait and see what would happen next.

A few days passed and I thought maybe she had decided to let it go. Janice and I continued to do everything as we had been doing, the only difference was if she heard a car door shut outside, it made her uneasy and I was upset that Debby had started all of this again.

One morning there was a knock at the door, Janice and I were a bit startled since neither of us had heard anyone pull in.

"That is odd Justus, who would be here so early, and why didn't we hear a car?" I cautiously went to the back door and looked out to see sheriff Clark.

"I didn't expect to see you this morning." I wasn't sure how to act, usually when I saw him it meant bad news.

"Justus, I seem to always be the bearer of bad news and I am sorry, but I have no choice, it is my job apparently." Janice came up behind me.

"What's wrong?" He looked at her and then back at me,

"I am afraid Justus is going to have to come with me, there have been some allegations that he was involved in a number of homicides." My heart began to race and my entire body seemed to go limp, Janice took hold of me and I could tell she wasn't going to let go.

"Homicides? That is ridiculous, who in the world would say a thing like that?" I had to act completely surprised and Janice chimed in as well, "who is telling such lies about him? He is a good man, why would someone try to implicate him in a crime?"

Tim just stood motionless and replied, "I am not at liberty to divulge that information, but there is some indication that this could be a complete fabrication." I noticed a deputy behind him all of a sudden.

"Sheriff, we need to cuff him for transport."

"No, that will not be necessary, I am sure Justus will come willingly."

"Of course I will, I want to get to the bottom of this as well." I got into the patrol car and looked back at Janice, "I am sure this will all be worked out in short order, I will call you when you can come pick me up." She just nodded her head and I could see the tears start to well up in her eyes as she quickly turned and went back inside.

We started toward the station and Tim began to speak.

"Justus, do you know a woman named Deborah Matteson?" I had to think for a split second, I had never thought of Debby as Deborah, but that must be her legal name.

"Yes, I dated her for a while, why do you ask?"

"She is the one accusing you of these crimes, normally we would dismiss it as a jealous lover or something of that nature, but she has given a lot of details and even given us a revolver she said was used in a couple killings." I was now officially frightened, with a gun it wouldn't be too hard to make a case, but it would be her word against mine I reasoned as to who pulled the trigger.

"Well I do know that she was abused by her ex and carried a gun, so that must be where it came from."

"Don't worry Justus, we will just have some questions for you to answer and then you can leave I am sure."

I wish that was all that happened that day, I had a feeling it was the beginning of the end and didn't know what to do. I decided to play dumb and act as if she were trying to get even with me for leaving her for Janice. I was questioned for a number of hours, at this point all they had was circumstantial evidence, but there was a lot of it. Debby had told them I was the 'Justice killer' and if that was the case it would gain a huge amount of media attention.

Sheriff Clark didn't want word to get out about this but still decided to book me for the record. He assured me this wouldn't get out of control and he would do everything he could to keep it quiet.

Debby had been released the day before and I started to worry about Janice. I was comforted that she didn't have the gun anymore at least.

"Justus, we also booked her in as an accessory to murder, I wanted her to know that this was no game and there would be consequences for her no matter what. If she is making false statements she will be punished."

His words gave me no comfort and I just wanted to go home.

I called Janice later that day from the jail when they finally released me on my own recognizance. As she came into the station the sheriff spoke.

"Justus, make sure you stick around in case I need to ask you some more questions." I of course agreed and Janice and I drove home.

"Oh my god Justus, this is horrible, you could go to prison if they have evidence." I tried to think of what they could possibly have, and hoped it was nothing.

"Don't worry darling, remember I am innocent until proven guilty!" I smiled at her and spoke in a overacted voice to try and lighten the mood, but I could tell she was as scared as I was.

"No matter what I am behind you and will be there for you as long as you want me to."

"I know, and we will get through this, I love you baby and always will."

"I love you too Justus, I have never stopped."

The next couple weeks went by with nothing out of the ordinary happening, I hoped that maybe Debby had possibly left the area since the sheriff told her she would be in trouble no matter what. It unfortunately was not the case and again early one morning there was a knock at the door.

"Morning sheriff, anything new with all of this?" Janice and I decided that I would deny everything to the end, no matter what there always had to be a doubt in the minds of others.

"Unfortunately Justus, there are some questions that need to be answered, you will have to come with us again. The chief is making me do this by the book so I will have to cuff you." A lump was in my throat and once again fear gripped me, Janice started to cry but the sheriff told her it would be alright and not to get upset.

We drove in silence for a bit and then he spoke.

"Justus, Debby has given us a lot of details and with the information we have from agencies out west it doesn't look good."

"I am not sure what she is saying, but even though we traveled together for a while, she slept different places at different times and I wasn't with her."

" I'm not saying she is telling the truth, but there are some circumstances that are not good right now. She has alerted some people in the media and we are going to have to keep you in the jail for a while, if for no reason other than your own protection." I had no idea why I would need protection, but as we neared the station I could see a large group of people out front.

"Holy crap, what are all those people doing there?"

"Like I said the news media has word that we might have the Justice Killer, and it is a big deal." Getting out of the car there was a rush of reporters around me. "Are you the Justice Killer?"

"What made you turn to violence?"

"Were you abused as a child?" There were a dozen people all screaming questions at me, I put my head down so they couldn't see my face and stayed close behind the sheriff as he and other men pushed through and got me inside.

"This is probably not going to end anytime soon, and you will have to stay here until the judge sets bail, I will let you call Janice if you like, I know she has been there for you since your mom passed away." I thanked him as they led me to my little cell.

It was like being in a movie; here I was in a tiny room with pale yellow walls, a bed, and toilet/sink combination. It was cold and hard, and I wanted to go home to Janice.

I was brought before the judge the next morning and told I would have an attorney supplied for me if I couldn't afford one, Janice and I had some money saved up but I knew that an attorney would bankrupt me, so I agreed to have a public defender. The judge also declined to set bail at this time, at least until the media frenzy had died down, and that was not going to happen. Tim let me talk with Janice and allowed her to come see me once in a while even though he didn't have to. The D.A. said he had overwhelming evidence and didn't want to allow bail, as there was fear of me fleeing.

"If he is indeed the Justice Killer, he is implicated in over 50 murders, we cannot take the chance of flight." The judge agreed and I stayed where I was.

Janice told me how reporters had been to the house multiple times but she only insisted on my innocence and told them to leave. I hated that she had to put up with all of this and wished I could go back to the time when we were first together.

I had to appear in court every few days and listen to whatever evidence was presented against me. As I suspected mostly it was circumstantial, at least until the day I saw Debby again. She had also been in the jail this whole time, but I was unaware of it. Looking at me, her eyes were like that of a mannequin, lifeless and without the sparkle that was once there. I felt pity for her for a moment, until she began to speak. She told of the men I had killed, how we found them, and plotted how they would die. Then she said the thing that sickens me to this day.

"I wanted to stop, but Justus said if I tried to leave he would kill me too."

I was stunned and jumped up to defend myself, "I would never raise a hand to a woman..." My attorney pulled me back and covered my mouth telling me that I was only implicating myself more as a man that hated abusive men. I knew he was right and sat there listening as she made me sound like one of the monsters I had eliminated.

On the days that I was not in court I could watch TV and the news always had something to say about the trial. I realized that I had a lot of activists and women's groups behind me. There were interviews with psychologists that supposed my crimes had to do with my abusive upbringing, women that said their group "supported extreme measures like what The Justice killer had done", and that if more women took the law into their hands abuse would be a thing of the past. I also saw interviews with men that said I was nothing but a psycho and should be killed the way I had murdered those other men. Overall I knew most people were behind me, but I was kept away from any other prisoners that were brought in, for my own protection I was told.

I realized this was true when one night I heard a voice from the cell next to me, "Hey shit head, if I could get over there I would give you a beating like the one I gave my wife today, then I would smash your head through the bars of your cell." I didn't say a word, but knew there was no doubt he would have made good on his words. I started to get depressed to the point of not caring anymore, I hadn't done anything to help anyone really. Abusive pieces of crap like him were never going to go away.

I know if it weren't for Janice always being there for me I would have committed suicide by now I am sure.

The trial continued and so did the media circus, I do believe that in some ways it at least brought domestic violence out of the shadows and got more people involved to help the victims.

Anyway, I am not going to bore you with all the details of the trial, it went on for weeks that seemed like years, now it has been years. As you well know I was convicted of five of the killings and sentenced to life in prison without a chance for parole. Debby was convicted as an accessory to murder and given 20 years. Janice, true to her word has stuck by me; she visits whenever she is able and keeps me from taking my life to this day.

So Father, that is how I have come to be here talking with you now, God is still a mystery to me, but I am hoping you know more than I do about him.

"Your story is amazing to me to say the least my son, I have read your case and am familiar with many of the details. I cannot of course condone violence in any form, but I do now understand what led you to this prison a little better. I am also curious, you have been here for quite some time now, but this is the first time you have ever asked to speak to me, why is that?"

"As you might have gathered from my story I have never believed in God, and if he is there I always wondered why he allowed so many good people to suffer."

"In this world there is always injustice my son, but it has to be this way so we can prove what kind of people we really are."

"I think that is very unfair to put it mildly, but I have always known that life is not fair. Anyway the reason I decided to speak to you is because of a dream I have been having over and over lately. In the dream I am in a kind of fog, on one side I can hear the voices of the men I have killed screaming for me to come to them so they can have their revenge. Along with their voices are others more sinister asking for permission to take me. On the other side of me, I hear women's voices saying not to let them take me. I have saved them and they now want to save me. I wake up from these dreams soaked in sweat, they won't stop and I am afraid to sleep. I think I am going crazy."

"You are not going crazy, even as you have sat here these many years you have known the general prison population would have killed you long ago. These might be some of the voices you hear as you sleep. To the women you freed from the violence you are a savior to them the way Christ is a savior to me. I can't interpret your dream, but only ask if you think you helped anyone to have a better life?"

"Yes I do, but at the cost of my own life." He looked at me and put his hand on his cross, I realized that Jesus had also made a sacrifice at the cost of his life, and although I would never put myself on that level, it did make me feel better.

"Son, you have committed serious crimes, and we all have to pay for what we have done, but I think there are many who consider you a hero and thank you everyday for the freedom you gave them."

"I am not sure if I am comforted by that as I sit alone here day after day, but I do feel better. You are one of the few that knows for sure I am guilty of my crimes, but I guess that doesn't matter much now, at least my life is predictable!"

Justus laughed for a minute as the priest got up and was let out of the cell. He had always known that if the main population in the prison ever knew the extent of what he had done it wouldn't be long before a trustee allowed someone to get to him. As long as there was doubt, he had at least some on his side. He thought for a minute how he might possibly get a good nights sleep for once, but as he drifted off he heard the bars open. Jumping up in the dim light he was instantly subdued by a number of men, he struggled but was soon unconscious.

OUT THE DOOR

Justus awoke to find himself in the living room of a very nice house. His head was throbbing and it took a minute to focus but there was a glass of water, some aspirin, a video and a note on the coffee table in front of him. As he tried to figure out what had happened he looked around the room and slowly reached for the water. For a brief minute he hesitated and wondered if this really was aspirin and water, or if that was just an assumption on his part. "What the hell" he muttered as he downed them and drank the glass dry.

Picking up the note he started to read, "watch this video, you will no doubt recognize me, but the man is a stranger to you. He is my husband. After you have watched it read the back of this note, please wait until you have watched the entire video before you continue."

For a minute he was tempted to read it, but prison life tends to make you follow directions and it just felt unnatural at this point. He was still in a daze, what was all this about? How did he get out of prison, and where exactly was he? He decided to take a look outside before anything else and see if anything was familiar. From the living room window the landscape looked about the same, the sky was the usual overcast it always seemed to be, and the trees were just as dead here as outside the prison walls. Suddenly he noticed something out of the corner of his eye, was that the same radio tower as outside the prison? He walked into the kitchen and to the east to get a better look.

"Well I'll be damned", sure enough it was and he could see the prison walls from where he stood.

"Ok, what's going on here?"

He noticed he said this rather loud and glanced around to see if anyone had heard him. The house was still quiet and he went back to the living room.

"Alright, time for a movie and some munchies!" he laughed as he put the video in the player. Ok this is boring, he thought as he looked at what appeared to be a shot from up high in the kitchen.

The camera seemed to be on top of the cabinets and aimed at an empty room. After about 20 seconds a woman came in and looked up straight at the camera lens.

"Holy shit!" The writer of the note was correct, he did recognize her and it was obvious she wanted him to. For a second he thought about just running from the room and out of the house, but then what? As he contemplated this, a man came into view on the video. He had never seen him before and assumed it was the husband from the note.

"What the hell are you doing in here?" The man bellowed as he caught site of her.

"I was just getting you a beer is all." This was not the tone or attitude he was expecting from her and couldn't figure out why this woman would take that kind of verbal assault.

"If I wanted you to get me a beer I would have told you to get me one bitch!" At this the man pushed her aside and walked to the refrigerator to get himself a beer.

Justus already didn't like this guy and his hatred was soon to grow strong. The man was a hulking ogre of a man with a balding head and fat gut. Although the woman was no model, she was way too good for this guy that was for sure. She stood back against the center island with her face away from the camera and the man walked around in front of her. Justus could see his stupid face and the smug look of power he felt he had.

"I had a shitty day, you had better make it improve right now." He couldn't see exactly what was going on, but was fairly sure the man had pulled his zipper down.

"Do it, or else!" The ugly man continued.

Are you kidding me!? Justus couldn't believe this man was talking to her like this, and waited to hear the rejection he knew was coming. But no, she slowly lowered herself and did what she was told as the bastard drank his beer and then poured what was left on her head. He then reached down and pulled her up by her hair, "you give the worlds worst head!" He said as he turned her around and pinned her against the counter. Tearing her pants down with a violent motion he pushed her head onto the counter top and proceeded to force himself into her. She looked up at the camera and he could see tears in her eyes.

Justus wanted to turn it off, but the note had said to watch the entire video and now knowing who this was he was compelled to do it. For the next 5 minutes he endured what amounted to a violent rape. This piece of shit man, the type which he had always despised, raped, verbally abused, and beat her with a spatula.

The tape then abruptly ended and he wondered what had been cut off, but thankful that he didn't have to see anymore. Going back to the note he now read the other side.

"As you can see my life has been this kind of hell for many years. I have wished him dead and come close to killing him on many occasions. Obviously I can never do that, and take the chance of being caught. I know who you are, and what you have done. I hold none of it against you and am going to give you the chance to start a new life, but first you have to do what I never could. Upstairs there is a wall safe behind the family picture, the combination is 27-9-12 there is a gun and $100,000 in cash inside of it. Make sure he is dead and the money is yours. There is also a suitcase with a passport, an airline ticket to La Paz Bolivia, and clothing for you to change into. Shave your face and head clean, as it was the day you were convicted. Leave the gun on the floor next to the body, destroy the note and video, and get the keys from the hook in the kitchen by the door to the garage. Take the car to the bus station and the bus to the airport. Your flight will be leaving at 5pm today; my husband will be home at 2, if you do not succeed in killing my husband, you will be caught before you ever get on the flight. If you do as instructed you will be a free man. I sincerely hope we can both be free of our prisons by tomorrow.

"Wow, this was unbelievable... Justus was stunned, but at the same time the thought of freedom was overwhelming. He sat there and thought for a minute, was this just a trap? But at the same time, what was there to lose? He had no problem killing this man and in fact would enjoy seeing him in pain.

As he walked up the stairs and looked down at the living room he noticed how it was all so perfectly arranged, so tidy, almost like a model home. It seemed like a huge contradiction from the violence that had been going on here for so long.

At the top of the stairs he could see into the master bedroom and the suitcase was on the bed as the note had said. There was a large portrait on the wall of her and him along with who he assumed were someone's parents.

"Glad there aren't any kids to have seen this shit" he said in a subdued voice.

He pulled the picture off the wall and tossed it to the floor, sure enough here was the safe. As he reached up to the dial he noticed his hands were shaking, "hmmm... haven't felt this rush in a while." Funny how prison had dulled him so much he thought, how the only emotions were despair and fear. Why couldn't he open this safe??? Did he have the numbers right? Suddenly he felt like he was back in high school and trying to open that damn locker again while everyone else seemed to have no problem. Just then he got it right and swung open the door. The gun was on top, it was a small caliber revolver and under that was the money. There were other papers and envelopes but he was not

a thief and didn't even care what was in them. He looked at the clock by the nightstand and saw he had 2 hours before the husband returned home. Leaving the safe open and the picture on the floor he went to the suitcase and opened it up. On top was a passport, picking it up he opened it and smiled when he read his new name, "James Walken" she had done her homework. The picture was from the day he was admitted to prison, clean-shaven face and head. The airline ticket was also on top and he set it aside as he reached for some clean clothes.

The master bathroom was clean and roomy, large mirrors were on 2 walls, which would make it easy to see that his head was smooth. Rummaging through the drawers he found a scissors and some razors. He hadn't looked in a mirror for a while and thought briefly that he looked like Charles Manson, and immediately started to cut it all off. Getting into the shower and having the water hit his head and face again felt good, he had not really noticed how he had become numb to so many feelings that could make a man feel alive. He dried off and got dressed, cleaning up the hair meticulously and flushing it down the toilet. He glanced up and saw the man he was years ago, and almost even saw the boy that had died so long before.

"I wonder what it would have been like to have a 'normal' life" he muttered as he looked away.

None of that mattered now, he was going to be free or he would die trying. Walking back into the bedroom he noticed he had an hour left, he put the gun in his belt behind his back and walked down the stairs. In the kitchen he looked up at where the camera had been and then to the refrigerator.

"Maybe I should dump all his beer out on the floor" he briefly thought as he looked in, but he was hungry and instead grabbed a piece of leftover pizza.

Sitting on a stool at the island he at that moment could see her in the video, pressed against the counter and the tears in her eyes. Suddenly he was angry and threw the pizza against the wall and walked upstairs. He sat on the nightstand and faced the door waiting for the time to pass.

THE END OF FEAR

A short while later Justus heard the sound of a car pulling in, he was temped to get up and look out but decided to stay put and not take the chance of being seen. He could hear the footsteps who he assumed was the husband walking into the kitchen.

"How the hell did this pizza get here? Damn woman never cleans anything up!" A beer popped open and he could hear the footsteps coming up. He felt once again the adrenaline rush as his hand tightened on the gun behind his back.

Suddenly there he was, at first he only noticed the picture on the floor, then the safe. Catching sight of Justus he blurted out in an angry voice, "I don't know who you are, but you are about to die." Justus only smiled as he pulled the gun from behind his back, "No, I think that honor goes to you."

The mans entire demeanor changed abruptly and like so many other bullies he had seen in his life, this one also became a coward.

"Please don't shoot me, I have a wife that needs me to take care of her."

This was too much for Justus to hear and he gritted his teeth and with hatred in his voice continued, "yes, I know you do, I have seen how you treat her. Do you know who I am?"

"No, and I don't care, you can take the money and go, I won't give the cops a good description of you or anything."

"You incredibly miserable pile of horse shit, I am The Justice Killer, and you are about to feel justice." He fired a shot into the man's thigh and as he fell to the ground writhing in pain, Justus walked closer.

"How do you like to be in pain? Ever think of how your wife feels when you abuse her?"

With that he fired again, this time through the man's hand.

"I want you to know pain, and more importantly before you die I want you to know your wife is the one who sent me to you. The man struggled against the pain and spoke for the last time.

"I hope I see you in hell." The last shot went through his skull, Justus walked to the bed picked up the suitcase and replied, "I have already been there, and am not going back."

The instructions were to leave the gun, and destroy the note and video. He dropped the gun and walked back down the stairs. Picking up the video and the note he started put them in the fireplace but hesitated, if he kept them it would be leverage against her if she tried to change her mind. Quickly he put them in the suitcase and headed for the garage.

It felt wonderful to once again be behind the wheel, to have the freedom of the open road. Time was going fast and as he got off the bus knew he would have to run to make the flight. In a way it would be better he thought to be able to just get right to the plane and not have to sit around an airport waiting and worrying. As he neared the gate it was as if the area was deserted, the lady at the counter spoke up, "If you are going to La Paz you had better hurry! You almost missed this one!" She chuckled as she said this while he pulled out his ticket and passport.

"Well Mr. Walken, enjoy your flight." He walked quickly down the narrow corridor to the plane seeing a flight attendant at the door. Every turn he kept expecting to see police, but there were none there.

"Good afternoon sir, please take your seat we will be taking off shortly." Walking through the crowded plane he realized he had an aisle seat and remembered how the last time he had flown how much he wanted to be able to look out the window. Maybe this time whoever was sitting there would trade with him. Getting close to his row and putting his bag overhead he finally sat down.

"OH My God.... Justus!" His head snapped to his side as his mouth fell open, "Janice!!! How did you get here?" He couldn't believe what he was seeing, here he was next to the woman he loved so much, the woman that had waited all these years for him. Both of them didn't say a word, but embraced each other as tears of joy filled their eyes.

"Janice my sweet darling, what is going on? Is this all a wonderful dream for once?"

"This is not a dream my love, it feels like it to me as well though."

"How did you get here?"

"I was at home a couple nights ago and the ticket for this flight was delivered to me by some woman I have never seen before. She told me to be on this flight and everything I ever wanted would be mine, that I could once again be happy. I wasn't sure I believed her, but had to come here and see what was going on, something in her voice made me trust her, and I know the ticket was expensive."

"Was she somewhat stocky, short brown hair, and glasses?"

"Justus, how could you possibly know that?" He thought back to the video, and could picture her now, but in his mind she was now smiling.

"Janice, you aren't going to believe this, but she is the warden at the prison!" I have a lot to tell you, but she was right, we can be happy now, and so can she."

"I am not sure what to think of all of this, but I know I have spent a lot of my life afraid. At first I was afraid of my husband, of what he would do to me each day. Then I was afraid I would ruin your life if you knew I was carrying your child. After that I was once again afraid I would lose you forever in that prison. I decided I wouldn't be afraid again, that I would do what it took to be brave and maybe have the chance for real happiness. In my wildest dreams I couldn't have imagined this. Maybe all those women you helped were there telling me to have courage and faith. I hope someday I have the chance to tell other women to have courage and faith as well, life can turn around and there can be love and happiness."

As Justus held her in his arms he thought about everything that had happened since the fateful day that he decided to free his Mom from the abuse she endured, about all the women and children he tried to give a new life to, and these last long years.

Would he do it all again? Did it make any difference at all? There is really no way to know, but now that you know his story, you need to ask yourself some questions... How is my life? Can I make it better? Am I tired of being afraid? Life is too short to spend it in fear, live the life you have. Be courageous, and don't forget... Justus could be just around the corner.